"Come On. You're Wet Clear Through. Let's Get You Home."

Vince held out his hand to Christy. She willingly allowed him to help pull her to her feet, but when he swept her up off the ground and into his arms, she protested, "I can walk!"

"Of course you can." Vince didn't put her down. "You're capable of doing anything you want to do."

She put her arms around his neck and wove her fingers together, merely a means of steadying her precarious position, she told herself. "You're making fun of me. Where's Muffin?" she asked, looking around for the little terrier who had caused the entire escapade. "You naughty boy," Christy scolded.

"Am I a naughty boy, too?"

Christy looked at Vince. Their faces were an inch apart. "I think you like that idea," she accused.

A grin tugged at his lips. "Sometimes naughty is nice."

Dear Reader,

Happy holidays! At this busy time of year, I think it's extra important for you to take some time out for yourself. And what better way to get away from all the hustle and bustle of the season than to curl up somewhere with a Silhouette Desire novel? In addition, these books can make great gifts. Celebrate this season by giving the gift of love!

To get yourself in the holiday spirit, you should start with Lass Small's delightful *Man of the Month* book, *'Twas the Night*. Our hero has a plain name— Bob Brown—but as you fans of Lass Small all know, this will be no plain story. It's whimsical fun that only Lass can create.

The rest of December's lineup is equally wonderful. First, popular author Mary Lynn Baxter brings us a sexy, emotional love story, *Marriage, Diamond Style*. This is a book you'll want to keep. Next, Justine Davis makes her Silhouette Desire debut with *Angel for Hire*. The hero of this very special story is a *real* angel. The month is completed with stellar books by Jackie Merritt, Donna Carlisle and Peggy Moreland—winners all!

So go wild with Desire, and have a *wonderful* holiday season.

All the best,

Lucia Macro
Senior Editor

JACKIE MERRITT

THE LADY AND THE LUMBERJACK

SILHOUETTE *Desire*

Published by Silhouette Books New York

America's Publisher of Contemporary Romance

SILHOUETTE BOOKS
300 East 42nd St., New York, N.Y. 10017

THE LADY AND THE LUMBERJACK

ISBN: 0-373-05683-4

First Silhouette Books printing December 1991

Printed in the U.S.A.

JACKIE MERRITT

and her husband live just outside of Las Vegas, Nevada. An accountant for many years, Jackie has happily traded numbers for words. Next to family, books are her greatest joy, both for reading and writing.

One

Christy Allen shivered with a chill that was as much internal as from the dampness she had picked up during her hasty trip from the Morrison Logging Company's office to the hospital. It was drizzling outside, with gloomy gray skies and the temperature somewhere in the fifties. At the frantic telephone call from her mother, Christy had dropped everything and made a mad dash for her car, not even slowing down for her jacket.

Her red-and-white-checked blouse had long sleeves but was only cotton, and even the heavier fabric of her jeans didn't seem to have enough substance to warm her fearful heart. She kept all of her dread to herself, however, maintaining a stern control of her emotions. Sitting with her mother, Christy held Laura Morrison's hand and offered consolation. "Joe will be all right, Mom. We must believe that."

Tears spilled from Laura's soft brown eyes. "I'm praying you're right, Christy."

Dr. Martin came into the small waiting room. He looked as he usually did, but Christy sensed more than professionalism in his sober demeanor. Joe was seriously injured, and the longtime family doctor couldn't gloss it over and pretend otherwise. "Hello, Christy. I'm glad you're here with your mother."

"Hello, Doctor."

Dr. Martin sat down beside Laura and took her other hand. "Laura, we're taking Joe to surgery. There's internal bleeding and we must locate its source."

Her mother was trying very hard to be brave, Christy knew, which was difficult for the older woman. Courage was not one of Laura Morrison's strong suits. She was a naturally timid, soft-spoken, gentle-hearted woman who was completely content with her role as homemaker and wife to Big Joe Morrison.

Laura and Christy had already been apprised of Joe's broken bones, his right leg and arm and three ribs, and Dr. Martin's latest information was almost more than Laura could take. Fresh tears filled her eyes, and she pulled both hands free to cover her face.

Christy met the doctor's troubled gaze, but she didn't want to question him in front of her mother. Joe was in good hands. Everything humanly possible was being done for him, and Christy knew she had to think of Laura and help her get through this. "Please keep us informed," she said quietly.

"I will. As soon as Joe's out of surgery, I'll be back to talk to you."

"Thank you, Doctor."

Alone again, Christy put her arm around her mother's shoulders. "Think positive, Mom," she murmured gently. "Joe will be fine. Keep repeating that in your mind."

Laura emitted a shuddering sob, then dropped her hands. "I need another tissue." Christy handed her one. "I was worried about Joe going up on the roof. But that leak in the kitchen was getting worse, and you know Joe. He just can't ignore anything that needs doing."

He should have hired someone to repair the roof instead of doing it himself, Christy could have said. Joe was well past sixty and not as agile as he used to be. With the roof wet and slippery he had lost his footing and taken a horrible fall.

Her own morning flashed through her mind. It was Saturday, and she usually spent Saturday mornings at the office. Joe normally went out to the logging site, but apparently this morning he'd decided to fix the roof instead.

Joe Morrison was Christy's stepfather, but she loved him as much as she loved the memory of her own father, who had died when she was nine. Untrained for anything else, Laura had gone to work as a waitress in Mabel's Café, which was where she'd met Joe. Christy was fourteen when her mother and Joe were married, and as gruff as Joe's personality was, he had never been anything but kind and affectionate to his stepdaughter.

Christy had been working for Joe, running his office and doing his bookkeeping, for five years now. After college she had lived in Seattle for several years, but during a vacation in her hometown she had learned that Joe's longtime secretary and bookkeeper had left the area several months before. The company records had been in an awful mess, and Christy had decided to move back to Oregon and help Joe out.

She had never regretted it. It was Joe who had paid for her education, which had been only one of his many generosities through the years. Christy had systematically organized the office and settled into a satisfying routine. She felt that she had come to understand the logging business extremely well and knew that Joe was well pleased with her work.

But that work was strictly white-collar, and sitting in the hospital waiting room with her mother, Christy was getting some glimpses of an uncertain future for the business. With

Joe laid up and facing a long recuperation at best, who would run the physical end of the business? Who would deal directly with the employees? Who was there to lead them the way Joe did?

It was another reason for dire concern on this terrible morning, another worry that Christy kept to herself. Laura had little interest in the business, nor did she understand it. But even if she knew exactly what was on Christy's mind, she was quite obviously in no mood to talk about contracts and logs and money.

"Would you like a cup of coffee, Mom?"

"Coffee?" Laura appeared too dazed to make even that simple decision.

Christy made it for her. Rising, she kissed her mother's cheek. "I'll run down to the cafeteria and get us both a cup. I'll only be a few minutes."

Starting for the open doorway, Christy picked up the sound of approaching footsteps. Heavy footsteps. Before she reached the doorway it was filled by a man.

Vincent Bonnell! What was he doing here? What weird coincidence had brought Joe's biggest competitor to this waiting room at this particular moment in time?

"Hello," he said, his eyes moving over her.

Christy had never spoken to this man before, but she had seen him any number of times. Completely avoiding anyone in Rock Falls was impossible, but the Morrisons and the Bonnells simply didn't mix. As the two biggest loggers in the area and rivals for the major timber contracts that the local sawmill handed out so sparingly, Vincent Bonnell and Joe Morrison left each other strictly alone.

Their men were a different matter. Every so often Bonnell employees and Morrison employees slugged it out in one or another of the local bistros, all in the name of loyalty to their particular boss, apparently. Such small-mindedness had always annoyed Christy, but because of her own loyalty to Joe, she had done her best to ignore the situation.

Facing Vincent Bonnell in such close quarters was rather overwhelming for Christy. First of all, he had always struck her—from afar, of course—as exactly the sort of man she stringently avoided. One go-around with an overly confident, overly macho man, a painful episode that had taken place before she'd moved back to Rock Falls, was quite enough for her. She had determined then, and still felt the same way, that she would rather live alone for the rest of her life than become involved with another man she couldn't trust. And Vincent Bonnell *looked* to be as untrustworthy as they came, if a massive dose of self-assuredness was any measure.

There was more to Christy's cautiousness than Vince's aura of self-confidence, of course. No one ever claimed that a simple hello was the start of anything personal between a man and a woman. But there was something else to consider in this startling encounter, primarily, just what the heck was Vincent Bonnell doing here? Christy couldn't help gaping at the man.

He was more her age than Joe's, a big, ruggedly handsome man with a shock of dark, nearly black hair and piercing gray eyes. Absorbing details of the man's exterior appeal against her better judgment, Christy recalled some of the things she'd heard about him. Vince, as he was called—among other things—was a second-generation logger. It was his father who had started the Bonnell Logging Company at about the same time Joe had started his business.

When Christy didn't immediately respond to his hello, Vince looked past her to Laura. "Hello, Mrs. Morrison."

Why, he was here because of Joe! Stunned, Christy moved aside to let him enter the room. He walked past her, leaving a scented trail, a not unpleasant smell of rain, damp clothing and maleness. Utterly bewildered, she watched him sink down on the chair next to her mother.

"I just heard about Joe. Is he all right?"

"He's in surgery," Laura whispered.

Christy saw Vince's head come about. "You're his daughter, aren't you?"

"Stepdaughter." Christy couldn't understand this. Since when did a Bonnell give two hoots about a Morrison?

Still, she couldn't deny the compassion in the man's eyes. It was all very mystifying.

Vince patted Laura's hand. "I'm sure he'll be just fine, Mrs. Morrison." He got to his feet. "May I have a few minutes of your time?" he asked Christy.

She blinked. "Why...I suppose so."

"Let's talk in the hall." Vince looked down at Laura for a moment, then swung around to the door. Christy followed him out of the waiting room. They both remained silent while they walked away from the area.

Matching his long strides was impossible. Christy barely came up to his shoulder, and her boots had two-inch heels. He was a mountain of a man, three or four inches over six feet and heavy in the shoulders and chest. His thighs were as big around as her waist, Christy thought irrationally.

Vince stopped and looked down at her. He'd seen her a lot of times, but not up this close, and he was realizing just how small she really was. What color were her eyes—gray or green? Some of each, he decided, turning his attention to her long mane of shimmering chestnut hair. A man could get lost in hair like that. "What's the real dope on Joe? Your mother's in no condition to talk about him, but you seem reasonably cool."

"Cool?" Christy's eyes widened defensively. "I'm hardly cool about it, Mr. Bonnell. But I wouldn't be much support to Mother if I broke down."

"Sensible attitude. How badly is Joe hurt?"

Christy cleared her throat. She couldn't have depicted this scene in her wildest imagination. "He has several broken bones, but I think Dr. Martin's more concerned with some internal bleeding. That's why Joe's in surgery."

"I heard he fell off the roof of his house."

"He did."

Shaking his head disgustedly, Vince looked away. "Why in hell would a man his age climb up on the roof in this kind of weather?"

Christy stiffened. She felt the same way, but Vincent Bonnell had no right to criticize *anything* Joe might do. "Just what is your interest in this, Mr. Bonnell?"

"Call me Vince. And there's nothing underhanded about my interest, Christy." He'd heard her name around town, just as she'd known who he was. But she wasn't his type of woman. He liked them long-legged and breezy, and Christy Allen was petite, probably introverted, *much* too serious.

Besides, Vince wasn't even positive she was pretty. Her facial features were rather sharp, as was her voice. He knew a few things about her, for one, her reputation for aloofness. She didn't inhabit the local bars, nor hang around the bowling alley, and the sporadic glimpses he'd gotten of her had been in restaurants, the post office, a grocery store.

Uncomfortable under Bonnell's bordering-on-rude scrutiny, Christy lifted her chin. "I was on my way to the cafeteria to get Mother some coffee. I really must get back to her. Thank you for stopping by."

She walked off, but it was only a second before Vince fell into step beside her. "What about Joe's business?" he inquired.

The blunt question startled Christy into an abrupt halt. If she was suspicious about Bonnell's interest, who could blame her? He had to know, as well as she did, that if Joe's contract with the sawmill wasn't filled in a timely manner, he would lose it.

And the likely candidate for a replacement contract was Vincent Bonnell!

Christy's stomach tightened. "What about it?" she asked defiantly.

Vince hesitated, then barged into exactly what she was daring him to get near. "Look, I know how Joe operates, because I do the same thing myself. Logging is a tough business. I'd bet anything that at least half of Joe's equipment is collateral for bank loans. Repairs and maintenance are a never-ending drain. Payroll and insurance costs keep going up. He's got a million dollars tied up in equipment, and probably less than twenty thousand in the bank. No work, no pay, and without logs delivered to the mill, you're not going to be able to meet Joe's financial obligations." He edged a little closer. "Joe could lose everything."

Breathing was suddenly a chore. Bonnell had so aptly described her own fears that Christy was momentarily speechless. She couldn't question his accuracy, either. He was in the same business and obviously dealt with the same pitfalls that Joe did on a daily basis. Get the logs to the mill, meet payrolls, meet the bank loans, pay this, pay that. But without log deliveries, and lots of them, there wouldn't be money enough to do anything with. Joe *could* lose everything.

Still, it seemed horribly disloyal to be discussing his business with Vincent Bonnell, of all people. "I realize the seriousness of the situation," she finally said coolly. "But I'm not going to panic about it, and it really is none of your affair, Mr. Bonnell. Now, if you'll excuse me?"

Again she walked away, only this time her legs weren't very steady. She couldn't believe it when Bonnell caught up with her with all the tenacity of a bulldog. "Joe runs his own crew, which means you don't have a qualified foreman now. My dad used to operate that way, too. He felt that no one else had the brains to oversee his operation, I guess. Joe's the same breed, stubborn as an old mule. You're high and dry, without a superintendent, Christy. And those yahoos Joe's got working for him—"

Christy spun. "Are no worse than the 'yahoos' you've got working for you! Joe's got some good men, Stubb Brannigan, Clem Molinski, Len—"

"Stubb's a heavy drinker. Clem's an old man. Len doesn't have the sense of a hummingbird."

"I'll figure something out," she said, anger mounting. "This discussion is over, *Mr.* Bonnell!"

Frowning, Vince watched her go. He'd really ticked her off, when all he'd meant to do was help. He knew she had worked for Joe for a long time, but he had wondered if she would understand what kind of mess Joe could be in with this accident.

Vince rubbed his jaw thoughtfully. Maybe she understood more than he'd given her credit for. She seemed bright and intelligent, if a little sharp-tongued. Maybe old Joe was damn lucky to have her in his office.

And she was kind of a surprise. Her looks, that is. Even in the few minutes they'd been together, Christy's high, prominent cheekbones and pointy little chin had seemed to grow in appeal. She did have great hair and bottomless green eyes. And just look at the sweet sway of that cute little behind! Funny, he'd never noticed before what a great walk Christy Allen had.

With a faint grin Vince turned down another corridor. The lady was understandably on edge right now. He'd keep tabs on Joe by calling the hospital later, and he'd work on the Morrisons' problem, too. Competitor or not, Joe didn't deserve to lose his business over a fall from a roof he'd had no business being up on.

At ten that night Christy wearily unlocked the front door of her small house. Muffin, her little tan-and-brown terrier, greeted her as usual, yapping and jumping around in circles. Christy bent down and scratched Muffin's ears. "You're hungry, aren't you, pal? Dinner's late by about four hours."

Christy straightened. "Come on, Muffin. Let's find you something special to eat to make up for the delay."

The day had been long and exhausting, and Christy was glad to be home. Not that closing herself into her own little domain would solve anything. Joe was still in serious condition, although, according to Dr. Martin, he had every chance of pulling through. "We'll monitor him in Intensive

Care for a few days because of his age. His system's had a bad shock.''

Laura had been tired and glad to go home, too. Even so, her parting words to her daughter had been about driving herself back to the hospital first thing in the morning. Christy knew that her mother would all but take up residence at the hospital until Joe could come home, which was perfectly understandable.

But she, as the sole caretaker of Joe's business now, didn't dare spend every waking moment at his bedside. After dropping her mother off, Christy had made a brief stop at the office to turn off the computer she'd left running all day. Tomorrow morning she would go in, finish up the work she'd started today, *then* go to the hospital. In the meantime she had the ICU's telephone number, so she could make periodic calls and check on Joe's condition.

Christy was no longer worried that Joe wasn't going to make it. He was a strong man with an iron will, and barring some unpredictable complication, Christy was confident that he would recover in time. But she didn't want him worrying about the business, nor did she want him recovering with the knowledge that everything he'd worked so hard for was going down the drain because of his accident.

It was up to her to see that the worst didn't happen, a brutal fact that had kept her stomach tied in knots all day.

After feeding Muffin and fixing a cup of tea for herself, Christy carried it to the bathroom and turned on the bathtub's spigots. While the tub filled she washed her face. The bright lights above the sink revealed clear skin and eyes that were maybe a tad too large for her small face. She would never be classified as a beauty, although certain men through her adult years had found her attractive. Unhappily the one big romance of her life had left some unforgettable scars. She had lived quietly ever since, by choice.

It wasn't that Christy didn't want romance in her life; it was that she hadn't met a man who was solidly placed, a man with substance and intelligence and purpose. Men who seemed to rely too much on their good looks and charisma automatically raised her guard. Somehow Bonnell appeared to fit that category, and frowning at herself in the mirror, Christy had to wonder about what could very well be only a snap judgment of the man.

The truth was, Vincent Bonnell's visit had bothered her all day for a number of reasons. Why would he go out of his way to show concern for Joe? To Christy's knowledge the two men had always avoided each other. Was Bonnell crass enough to be hoping for the chance to pounce on Joe's logging contract?

That seemed like such a disgustingly low thing for anyone to do, competitor or not, that Christy had a hard time accepting it. Still, she couldn't come up with any other reason why Bonnell would care if Joe was in the hospital, and the suspicion stayed with her, even while she pondered a strange personal awareness of the man. He wasn't her type or, more accurately, her *preferred* type. But few women wouldn't notice Bonnell's outstanding physique. He had really looked her over, too, and hadn't even attempted to camouflage the masculine analysis.

How had she measured up? Christy's eyes narrowed at her own reflection until she realized what she was doing. Then she jerked her chin in sudden vexation and turned away from the mirror. Whatever Vincent Bonnell's opinion had been, she didn't even want to think about it!

Christy was sure she wouldn't sleep well that night, but she conked out the minute her head hit the pillow and awoke, at seven the next morning, to the sound of rain on the roof.

Muffin was standing beside the bed, wagging his stub of a tail. Christy smiled at the cute little terrier. "Morning, pal." Muffin immediately jumped onto the bed, ready for his usual morning romp.

"Not this morning," Christy sighed, and lifted Muffin back to the floor. Actually, along with yesterday's crushing events, the fact that it was still raining was depressing. Not that rain in western Oregon was abnormal. But Christy had been longing for some sunshine, anyway, and the continuing gray skies seemed to accentuate the somberness of her situation.

And Joe's. And her mother's.

Wearing a worried frown, Christy got up. After calling the hospital and hearing that Joe was doing okay, she called her mother. "Did you sleep all right, Mom?"

"Better than I thought I would."

"That doesn't surprise me. Yesterday was exhausting. I should be at the hospital around noon. We can have lunch together if you'd like."

"That will be fine, honey. I'll be watching for you."

While Christy dressed and ate a bowl of cereal she wondered if she could talk about the business with her mother. By the time she left the house she had decided against it, however. Laura had enough on her mind right now, and in all honesty, probably wouldn't care what else happened as long as Joe recovered.

Rock Falls was drenched. The little town's wooden buildings were gray and dark with absorbed rain, its streets slick and puddled with standing water. Christy drove slowly and avoided the worst puddles. Traffic was Sunday-morning light, and she made it to the south edge of town, where the Morrison Logging Company's office was situated, without mishap.

Unlocking the front door, she went inside and immediately shivered in the damp, chilly building. After turning up the thermostat, Christy set her purse down and put on a pot of coffee to brew.

Then she sat down at her desk and stared at the silent computer. She had worked very hard to get the logging operation on the computer, and any phase of the business could be called up by the stroke of a few keys. No one could ask for a more efficient record-keeping system than she had devised for Joe. But what good were efficient records without income?

She was worried sick, Christy finally admitted, knowing that she had been afraid of this moment. It was reality time, time to face the fact that Joe wasn't going to come bounding through that front door today, nor tomorrow. Not for weeks, maybe even months.

The telephone rang, startling Christy. She grabbed it. "Hello?"

"Christy? Clem. What's this I hear about Joe?"

"He's in the hospital, Clem." Christy detailed the accident, explaining everything between Clem's commiserating comments.

But then it came, the question she had already been doing battle with: "Who's gonna run the job, Christy?"

She cleared her throat. "I've been . . . giving that some thought, Clem."

"Should we go to work in the morning?"

"Oh, yes! Please tell the other men. I'll figure something out, Clem. But please tell everyone to show up in the morning."

"Well, I guess so. I just don't know, though. Someone's gotta ramrod the job."

Christy spoke in a very small voice. "Do you think you could do it, Clem?"

"Me?" Christy winced through a long silence. Clem finally mumbled, "Well, I guess I could try."

"Oh, thank you, Clem. Get everyone working in the morning. Tell them about Joe's accident, and—"

Clem interrupted her gush of relief. "I'll do my best tomorrow morning, Christy, but you're gonna have to line someone else up." Clem's reluctance went right through Christy, although she also felt empathy with the aging man's wariness. His usual job of operating the boom, the huge crane that loaded logs onto the trucks, was only one phase of the operation and a far cry from complete responsibility.

Her worry had returned, and Christy spoke almost dully. "All right, Clem. I'll talk to you sometime tomorrow."

"Can Joe have visitors?"

"No one but family today. Check with the hospital, Clem."

Christy slowly put the phone down. Clem didn't want the job, and she couldn't fault him for it. There was so much to the operation—sawing the trees down, bucking and limbing, skidding them to the landing for loading, hauling them to the mill, seeing to the brush and slash. Sixteen men in all, sawyers, truck drivers, equipment operators, *plus* the equipment itself to oversee and keep running. It was a tall order.

It was also a problem that needed solving quickly. Someone in Joe's crew surely had the ability to run the operation. One by one Christy went through the employees by calling up their personnel files on the computer. Half were immediately eliminated because of inexperience, and when she got down to a final few, it was all too apparent that her best bet lay with Stubb Brannigan. Stubb had the maturity and experience, but like Bonnell had pointed out, Stubb drank too much.

Would Joe trust him with the operation? Lord, did she have a choice?

Deep in thought, Christy raised startled eyes when the front door opened abruptly. "Morning," Vince Bonnell said. He had an unusually deep, resonant voice, and the greeting seemed to reverberate throughout the small office.

Christy rose slowly. She couldn't even begin to guess at the reason for this intrusion. As far as she knew, Bonnell had never stepped foot in this office before. Despite an immediate bombardment of suspicions, she managed a reasonably normal, "Good morning."

Vince sized her up again. No jeans today. A teal pullover sweater and matching slacks. A white blouse collar at the wide neck of the sweater. Thick, glossy hair around her face. Just the right amount of makeup. Trim. Neat. Maybe Christy Allen *was* pretty.

"Hope I'm not interrupting anything," he said, moving closer to the desk.

Yesterday he'd been in well-worn work clothes; today he was shiny clean in snug jeans, a white shirt and a black leather jacket. He had remarkable eyes, Christy noted, deepset and the color of wet slate. Intelligent eyes. Somehow that observation was personally elating, a reaction that Christy found utterly ludicrous. She wasn't going to be affected by this man, no matter how often he barged into her life!

"I was finishing up some work I started yesterday." Which wasn't quite true. She had intended on doing that, but still hadn't gotten to it. The problem of a superintendent had superceded everything else.

Vince felt her curious gaze following him as he walked around the office. He stopped at a table laden with healthy green plants in front of an east window. "Nice touch," he murmured, and gave her a lopsided grin. "Your idea, I'll bet."

When she remained silent—and guarded—he walked over to her desk. "I talked to a nurse in ICU this morning. Joe seems to be coming along."

"Yes." Christy cleared her throat. "Mr. Bonnell, I really do have a lot of work to do."

His eyes narrowed on her. "More than you know, I suspect."

She resented that. "I think I'm aware of the situation."

"But are you aware of the solution?"

What solution? What was he talking about? If he'd come here to suggest he take over Joe's contract, he was barking up the wrong tree!

"Is that fresh coffee I smell?"

"What? Oh. Well, yes."

Vince smiled. "May I have a cup?"

He had strong white teeth, and his broad smile did something funny to Christy's insides. Why? she questioned. Why, when she didn't want one thing to do with this man, did his smile nudge her femininity?

She was remembering some of the things she'd heard about him, one of which was a nickname. Vince "Bull"

Bonnell. Did anyone call him that to his face, or was it meant derogatorily and spoken furtively? How had he come by it, his size, maybe? Or was it because he horned into other people's affairs with the tactlessness of the proverbial bull in a china shop?

Only innate good manners carried Christy across the room to the coffeepot. She quickly filled two cups and returned to the desk, holding one out to her unwanted and unwelcome guest.

"Thanks."

He wasn't going to gulp it and leave, Christy finally acknowledged. And he appeared to be waiting. She caught on, and sank down onto her chair. He had the audacity to grin impudently at her while he sat down, too. "Now, let's have a little talk," he said in a tone that suggested they were really old friends and he had every right to be there.

"I don't know what you and I have to talk about," she exclaimed with some heat.

"We have quite a lot to talk about. I've figured out what you need to do to keep this business going during Joe's recuperation, and I think you're much too smart not to hear me out."

Two
―

Astonishment glued Christy to her chair. "*You've* figured it out? Did anyone ask you to work on the problem?"

Vince sat back. "At least you recognize that you have a problem."

Christy set her cup down, hard enough that a splash of coffee landed on some papers. She wiped it away with a glare across the desk. "Of course I recognize a problem. But just why is it your concern?"

"You still think I'm up to something, don't you?" Vince took a swallow of coffee and then set his cup down, too. He leaned forward and grinned. "What makes you so suspicious, honey?"

Drawing herself up indignantly, Christy rewarded his familiarity with a murderous look. How dare he presume she would accept that sort of masculine superiority? Yesterday's hasty assessment of Vincent Bonnell had been right on the money: the man was full of himself! "If you expect this conversation to go any further, don't call me honey!"

Vince's hands came up. "Whoa, little lady. Simmer down there. I didn't mean to rile you."

Groaning, Christy felt her temper draining away. "Little lady" was almost as bad as "honey," but obviously this man employed silly labels as a matter of course in his conversations.

Well, he was aggravating and irritating. But, perversely, he was also extremely attractive. If she had one ounce of good sense, she would firmly show Mr. Vincent Bonnell the door.

But what if he *did* have some kind of solution in mind for her dilemma? Dare she risk not hearing it? She was in no position to overlook any possibility, after all.

"Please get on with it," she said, concealing her impatience. Vince Bonnell affected her in peculiar ways, but the fact that he "affected" her at all was the most disturbing aspect of this whole disturbing situation.

"Sure will. I didn't come over here to upset you. I've been thinking about you and Joe and what's going on, and there's only one logical solution to your problem. You."

"Me," Christy parroted tonelessly, completely missing his meaning. "I don't understand."

"I have a feeling you know this business inside out, and I know for a fact that you don't have even one employee who's really capable of supervising the job. Who better is there to take Joe's place?"

Christy sat back, utterly aghast. "You're not suggesting I go into the woods!"

"Don't look so shocked. There are women loggers."

"Not very many."

"Look, I'm not saying you should pick up a chain saw or grease a 'dozer. But you could orchestrate the operation, which is what Joe does, and what my foreman does for me."

Christy was staring at him as though he had suddenly sprouted another head. "I don't believe this. If *that's* your brilliant solution..."

Frowning, Vince got to his feet. "Make fun of it if you want to, but it *is* a brilliant solution. I would loan you my man, but I need him myself. Besides, I think we both know that wouldn't work."

Christy stood up, too, inexplicably angry. "Oh, that's right. Let's not forget the childish feud your men and the Morrison employees just adore being a part of. What I'd like to know is, who started that moronic antagonism? This whole town is divided! Either you're a Morrison supporter or a Bonnell supporter, and never the twain shall meet!"

"I think that opinion is slightly exaggerated," Vince rebutted mildly. "Competitiveness isn't a bad thing, Christy. Loggers work hard, and if they let off a little steam now and then by taking a potshot at the competition..."

"Oh, give me a break," she scoffed. "Punching one another out is hardly a 'potshot' at the competition!"

Studying her, Vince picked up his cup and finished off his coffee. "How'd we get on that subject? Know what I think? You're as bad about that old feud as anyone else. You don't want to consider my idea because it came from me, a Bonnell."

"That's absurd. But so is your idea! In the first place, I hardly think those big, tough loggers would listen to a woman. You're all so macho, it's sickening!"

Vince felt as if he'd just been slapped. So much for trying to help this dizzy dame. Bright? Intelligent? Hah! Christy's narrow mind had turned a completely sincere suggestion into an insult. Well, he didn't need her or her damn problems! "Is that why you don't date anyone around here, because we're all so sickening?"

Christy's eyes blazed. "Don't get personal, Bonnell! My private life isn't on trial here."

"Neither is mine, lady. And you struck first!" Vince turned and started for the door. He stopped with his hand on the knob and an angry glint in his eyes. "You're letting your own inflexibility hamper your vision, lady. When you cool down, think about my idea. Without some direction, those men are going to have Joe's job in a helluva mess.''

"Why do you care?" she demanded as the door slammed behind him. Plopping down onto her chair, Christy sputtered for a moment, then jumped up to hurry to a window. She saw a muddy black pickup speeding away. "You jerk," she muttered, and watched until the truck turned a corner and disappeared from sight.

It was still raining, and she was so tired of gray drizzle that she wanted to scream. She was also so scared and worried that she wanted to cry, and the anger and fear within her were giving her a stomachache.

"Oh, God," she moaned hoarsely as she sat down at the computer again. This was a nightmare. No wonder she'd flown off the handle with Bonnell.

Still, arguing with the man the way she'd done was unbelievable. She couldn't even remember the last time she'd raised her voice to anyone. What was happening to her?

Nervously Christy ran her fingers through her hair, lifting its bulk back from her face. Her heart was pounding. Vince's anger was still in the room. Her own, too. She had behaved badly. Whatever Bonnell's motives were, *she* had behaved like a shrew. Worry was destroying her self-control, and yes, she might have plenty of reasons to be leery of Vince Bonnell. But yelling at anyone was inexcusable.

Realizing that it was close to noon, Christy shut down the computer, turned off the coffeepot and locked the office, every movement unsteady because of her trembling hands.

Laura was smiling when Christy arrived at Joe's room in ICU. "He was awake for a few minutes," Laura related gratefully. "He's going to be fine, I just know he is."

Joe was bandaged and casted and looked like hell, but Christy had enough sense not to say so. "Yes, he is, Mom. Just fine."

Leaving word with the floor nurse that they would be in the cafeteria, mother and daughter made their way through the hospital's corridors. "I was thinking about Vincent Bonnell coming by yesterday. That was very thoughtful, don't you think? I didn't know he and Joe were friends," Laura said.

Christy drew a shaky breath. She didn't want to talk about Bonnell, nor even think about him. For one thing, she felt deeply and searingly humiliated over their silly argument. For another, she didn't trust him. Actually, the list of reasons why she should avoid the man was growing by leaps and bounds. "They're not friends, Mom."

"Why else would he stop in to ask about Joe?"

Christy couldn't bring herself to get into that disturbing speculation with her mother. Bonnell's seemingly generous spirit could only be selfishly incited. There was no other answer for his abrupt about-face, no matter how it might look to Laura. Besides, even Bonnell's name made Christy cringe. She hoped that she never, ever had to face the man again.

She deliberately changed the subject. "Clem Molinski called the office this morning. He'd heard about the accident and wondered if Joe could have visitors."

"Joe will be pleased to see any of his men when he's able."

"I told Clem to check with the hospital. I'm sure when Joe's in a regular room he'll be able to have any number of visitors. They're just very particular in the Intensive Care Unit."

"Family only," Laura agreed.

In the cafeteria they selected dishes, paid for them and found a table. "Christy, are you going to be able to handle things while Joe's laid up?" Laura asked, surprising her daughter.

As she transferred plates from her tray to the table, Christy's common sense battled with an urge to be totally honest. Unquestionably it would feel wonderful to speak her mind, to just let go and lay out her fears and concerns for the future of Morrison Logging Company.

But how would upsetting her mother help the situation? In fact, if Laura really caught the scope of the problem, she would probably go into an emotional decline. And it would do no earthly good.

"I'll handle it, Mom. Please don't worry about the business. You have enough on your mind right now."

Laura smiled her sweet smile and reached across the table to pat her daughter's hand. "You're such a smart woman. I'm so proud of you, Christy. Joe is, too, you know. He can't praise you enough."

"I know," Christy said quietly. She couldn't get rid of Vincent Bonnell's shocking suggestion—along with a massive dose of remorse—and it remained only a millimeter behind every other thought. It was ridiculous, of course. How on earth would she manage a logging crew? Sixteen rough men? Just the idea was demoralizing.

By the time lunch was finished, Christy had decided to talk to Stubb Brannigan. With Clem's all-but-outright refusal to get involved, Stubb was really her only hope.

She left the hospital with the excuse of feeding Muffin and drove to Stubb's house. He was a bachelor, and Christy saw immediately that his battered blue pickup was absent. She drove on past the house and turned down Rock Fall's main street.

Watching for Stubb's truck, Christy finally spotted it parked near the Way Inn, which was a tavern with a rowdy reputation and certainly not the kind of place she ordinarily frequented.

Nevertheless, she found a parking slot and forced herself to walk through the tavern's front door. The smell of beer and cigarette smoke nearly staggered her. Music blared from some kind of unseen equipment, and the voices and laughter were almost as deafening. There were several nice bars in the area, but the Way Inn was definitely not among them.

Christy scanned the crowd of mostly roughly dressed, burly men from an uneasy stance just inside the door. When she saw Vincent Bonnell shouldering a path through a group of people, she was stunned. Was this the way he spent his Sunday afternoons? Why was fate throwing them together again? Christy's insides seemed to shrink into a small ball of misery. She wasn't prepared to see Vince again so soon after that exhibition of anger in her office.

"I hardly expected to see you here," he said coolly, unknowingly paralleling Christy's embarrassed thoughts. He had only stopped in to speak to a couple of his men, and Christy Allen walking in was the surprise of the century.

His patronizing attitude instantly reduced Christy's self-criticism. The man riled her. Damn it, he *affected* her! He caused sparks; there was no other explanation for the personality change she underwent in his presence. "I could say the same," she retorted, bringing her gaze from Vince to the crowd. At least he didn't seem to expect an apology! "I'm looking for Stubb. Is he here?"

"I haven't seen him, if he is."

"His pickup is parked outside."

Vince shrugged. "I guess he could have gone off in someone else's car. I was just leaving." He stared at Miss Prissy Christy for a long moment, wondering just what the hell was her big draw. Standing there knowing what a pain in the neck she was, and even reliving that idiotic argument in her office, he felt some kind of crazy urge to look after her. Why? She wasn't incompetent, even if his idea about her taking over Joe's job had shocked her socks off.

Well, she didn't belong in the Way Inn. That was one point that didn't need debate. He took Christy's arm. "Come on, I'll walk you to your car."

His brusqueness left no room for argument. But Christy was glad to get out of there and allowed his grasp until they were outside in the rain. Then, shaking off his big hand, she made a dive for her car door. Before she could close it behind her Vince took hold of it and leaned over to see in. "I take it that you're thinking about giving Stubb the foreman's job?"

"I have no choice." She shot him a defiant look. "Despite your suggestion to the contrary," she added before he could.

Vince eyed her thoughtfully. Maybe she was right. A bookkeeper's mentality was really beyond his ken. She was probably as sharp as a tack with figures, but dealing with numbers and people were two vastly different things. Maybe she was no match for a logging crew. They could be pretty rough sometimes, although, for the most part, loggers were polite and respectful around decent women.

And there was no doubt in his mind that Christy Allen was a decent woman. Which made him wonder about the very noticeable sizzle he was feeling. She was sexy as all get out, wasn't she? Yes, she was different from the women he normally admired, but she was reaching him all the same. What did she do in her free time? For fun? She had to have friends. Who were they?

"I guess you'll do what you want," he finally told her. Then he added, "I'm sure you'll discover the lay of the land soon enough by your own methods. But remember something, okay? If you run into a snag, don't hesitate to give me a call. I'm in the book."

Jerking his jacket collar up against the rain, Vince walked away, leaving Christy to stare after him. He was a surprising man, and she truly didn't know how to take him. One minute she was swamped with mistrust and the next she felt his sincerity.

But it was all so strange, a weird assortment of advances and retreats. Why was he bothering? She hadn't been receptive to his suggestions, nor even particularly kind. Christy gnawed on her thumbnail, frowning about the matter.

Well, God only knew where Stubb was, and sitting there trying to figure out Vince Bonnell was only adding frustration to her roster of ragged emotions. Christy forced herself to concentrate on Stubb.

He would show up for work tomorrow, she felt, so maybe she would have to drive out to the logging site in the morning and catch him there. That might be a good idea, anyway. She could talk to the whole crew then and give them the real facts of Joe's accident.

Starting the car, Christy headed for home. She really did have to feed Muffin, and then she would go back to the hospital and spend the evening with her mother.

The first thing Christy noticed upon awakening the following morning was the silence. The rain had stopped. Jumping out of bed and going to the window, she pulled the curtain aside. Sunshine!

With her spirit a hundred times better just because of a few feeble rays of sunshine, Christy began to prepare for a busy day. She had a dozen things to do at the office, but she would only stop in briefly, then head for the logging site. Her primary project for the day was talking to Stubb, and everything else would have to wait until that was behind her.

Christy recognized the ache in her stomach as anxiety. She'd taken it to bed with her last night and hadn't slept very well because of it. And she knew she wasn't going to get rid of it until she had something concrete accomplished with the logging crew.

It was a good hour's drive to the logging site, but before she left town she exchanged her compact sedan for Joe's four-wheel-drive pickup. After days of rain, the mountain roads would be muddy, and she didn't want to chance getting stuck. Following a few words with Laura, Christy finally got started.

The sunshine wasn't going to be a permanent fixture, Christy noted from a bank of freshly gathering clouds. But any break in dreary weather—however brief—was welcome, and at least the highway was relatively dry.

The secondary road she had to turn onto was a different matter. Slick and gooey, Christy was relieved that she'd had the foresight to take Joe's pickup. She slipped the gearshift into four-wheel drive and proceeded cautiously.

It had been a while since she'd been out there. Periodically Joe insisted she visit the logging site and see for herself what she so diligently recorded on the computer. But it had been a month since her last trip, and then it had been with Joe doing the driving.

The mountains were beautiful. The dark green forest was still dripping water, and the sunlight was making rainbows in patches of mist. Christy saw several deer, and despite the slippery road, found the drive pleasant.

There was a final turn onto a quarter-mile stretch of crude road that led directly to the logging site. Christy stopped the pickup and studied it with some trepidation. Rutted and oozy with mud, the road looked ominous. But she could tell that it had been recently traveled, which indicated to her that the crew had managed to get to work that morning.

She hesitated about getting started again, admitting that she didn't feel at all easy about this trip to the woods. Even just talking to the crew as a whole was out of her league. In many ways she was a loner, a woman who was perfectly comfortable with only her own company. She didn't seek crowds, nor need other people to enjoy herself. She was no good at making speeches, and actually viewed such an event as horrifying.

But this had to be done, and there simply was no one else to do it.

Drawing a deep breath, Christy stepped on the gas and started the pickup moving again. She was almost to the end of the road, heading into a sharp, ascending curve that wound around a jutting hillside, when she saw the logs. Like a dropped handful of giant matchsticks, the logs crisscrossed one another and completely blocked the roadway.

Christy's heart jumped into her throat and she braked reflexively. The pickup skidded sideways. Christy let up on the brake, got control of the truck, then braked with more caution. The pickup stopped just scant inches away from the nearest log.

Her heart was hammering from the near miss, but just as unsettling was the scene she could see through the windshield. The men were scrambling over the logs toward her, and just over the bank, at the left side of the road, a Morrison truck looked twisted and dented.

Her door was jerked open. "Are you okay?" Clem asked anxiously.

"I'm fine. Who was the driver? Was he hurt?"

A man stepped forward. "I'm the driver, Christy. This darn road is as slick as glass."

Moe Griffin didn't even have a visible scratch, and Christy breathed a sigh of relief. "Apparently this just happened."

"About twenty, thirty minutes ago," Moe affirmed. "A couple of the men are up at the site, getting a 'dozer to push the logs out of the way."

Christy climbed up onto a log to get a better view of the diesel logging truck. "How badly is it damaged?"

"She starts—I already tried it—but she won't be hauling logs for a few days," Moe replied gloomily. "Her underpinnings are all bent to hell."

"Underpinnings?"

"Frame," Clem clarified.

Morrison Logging Company owned five diesel trucks. Any one of them down for extensive repairs was costly business, not just because of new parts and labor, but every undelivered load of logs decreased income.

Moe looked despondent. That truck was assigned to him, and until it was functional again his paycheck would be next to nothing.

Too bad Moe wasn't superintendent material, Christy thought. The man was a good, dependable truck driver, but that was his only area of expertise.

Well, this was a fine mess. Christy looked around with a troubled expression. "How many other trucks went out this morning?" she asked, and caught the glances exchanged by some of the men.

Clem spoke up. "This was the first load, Christy. Things didn't go real well this morning."

This was a bad beginning: no deliveries and a truck accident. Christy knew that if she gave in to the throbbing weakness inside her worried body, she just might— No, she would do nothing but stay right here and attempt to untangle the situation. Or at least try to understand it.

Then it occurred to her that Stubb wasn't among the group of men she was looking at. She was still standing on the log, and she jumped down to the muddy ground. "Where's Stubb?"

Clem shook his head. "He didn't show up. We were just talking about that. No one's seen him since Saturday night."

"But his pickup was parked near the Way Inn yesterday afternoon," Christy said.

"That's where he was Saturday night," one of the men responded. "When I left, he was still there."

"He was still there when I left, too," another man put in.

"Well, that's strange," Christy said thoughtfully. "This isn't like Stubb, is it? I mean, according to my daily work sheets, Stubb rarely misses work."

One of the men laughed. "He might have a king-size hangover, but he always gets here."

"Hmm," Christy murmured. Maybe Stubb's old pickup had broken down and he'd left it on the street Saturday night. Maybe he'd been home yesterday, after all.

But why wouldn't he have caught a ride to work with one of the other men? Was he ill?

She would go by his house when she got back to town, Christy decided, and directed her attention back to the present disaster. "How long will it take to clear the road?"

The men were all wearing hard hats, and Clem lifted his, scratched his balding scalp and settled it back on his head again. "A couple of hours, I guess."

Until the road was cleared the logging job was literally fenced in. No other trucks could pass, which meant very few, if any, log deliveries today. Calamities of one kind or another were nothing new in the logging business, but Christy was beginning to get a more defined view of just what Joe did every day. He would know exactly what to do right now. He would be directing men and equipment in his gruff, no-nonsense voice. "Clem, you do this. Len, you do that."

Instead, the men were milling around—as Christy's insides were doing—with every single one of them looking slightly confused. Not that they didn't know the procedure needed to clear the road. Christy had only a vague idea of what it entailed, but most of the men knew what had to be done.

Only, no one was taking hold and assuming command. Christy looked at Clem, and she suddenly wanted to shake the old man. Clem had worked in the logging industry his whole life. Why didn't he have more gumption? More ambition?

Sighing, admitting that one couldn't change other people's personalities to fit their own needs, she realigned her thoughts and tried to speak without too much emotion. "I'm sure you all know about Joe's accident by now."

A rush of empathetic and sympathetic comments ensued. "Dr. Martin is optimistic about his recovery, but it's not going to happen overnight. I intend holding everything together during Joe's absence, but I need your help." Christy took a breath and a very big chance. "Clem has agreed to act as foreman until I can find someone else," she said, praying that Clem would back her up.

"Not a Bonnell man!" someone shouted.

Christy's eyes widened. "Who said that?"

"I did." A heavyset man with an enormous dark beard stepped forward. "I ain't working for no Bonnell man," he said belligerently. "And some of these other guys feel the same way."

Impatience rolled in Christy's stomach. Her dislike of public speaking deserted her in a rush of adrenaline. "First of all, I don't see any Bonnell man jumping up and volunteering for the job. Secondly..." She stopped herself from railing against that stupid feud. She wasn't going to change a years-old attitude by expressing disapproval and derision for it, especially when she strongly suspected that these men—and Bonnell's—thoroughly enjoyed the dissension. It was a game to them, and even Christy had to admit no one had ever been really hurt by it. It just seemed so darn silly to her.

Clem was standing by with a screwed-up face, blatantly ruffled over the announcement she'd made about him acting as foreman. *Oh, give me strength,* Christy silently prayed. She was making little progress here. Her best bet was still in locating and talking to Stubb. Heavy drinker or not—or maybe because of it, sad as that possibility was—the other men looked up to him.

"Clem, walk to the pickup with me, please," she said, not quite able to look directly into the crew members' eyes. She wasn't at all comfortable standing out here before these men, and it was again difficult to pretend otherwise. "Please get this road cleared as quickly as possible," she requested politely, then repeated something Vince Bonnell had said. "No work, no pay. Let's all try to remember that."

Clem shuffled over to the pickup with her, while the rest of the gang started climbing back to the other side of the spilled load of logs. "I'm sorry I put you on the spot, Clem. But until I talk to Stubb I just don't have anyone else."

The old man looked terribly unhappy, which weakened Christy's resolve a little more. "Just try to keep everyone working, Clem. That's all I'm asking."

She got into the pickup, turned it around and headed back down the mountain. And cursing accidents the world over did nothing but give her an alternative to bawling like a baby.

The telephone was ringing when Christy unlocked the office door, and she speeded up and ran for her desk. "Morrison Logging Company."

"Christy? Is Joe there by any chance?"

Recognizing the male voice as Rusty Parnell's, Rennard Lumber Company's timber supervisor, Christy's heart sank clear to her toes. Apparently news of Joe's accident hadn't yet reached Rusty, which was really her fault. She should have called him immediately. "Joe's in the hospital, Rusty. He had a serious accident."

"How serious?"

Christy cleared her throat. "He'll be out of commission for... a month." She knew it was going to be longer than that, but "a month" was all that came out of her mouth.

"A month! Who's taking over for him?"

Rusty was not only unsympathetic, he was instantly angry. "I'm working on it," Christy uneasily replied.

"I called because there haven't been any Morrison log deliveries today. Now I know why. Hell, this is a fine state of affairs."

"Rusty, things are at odds today, but everything will get back to normal. There'll be log deliveries tomorrow, I promise."

Rusty's voice gentled some. "Tell me what happened to Joe."

The man wasn't completely coldhearted. Only when it came to business. It was his job to see that Rennard's logging contracts were strictly adhered to, and he was a conscientious employee. Christy knew that Rusty could cancel Joe's contract and reissue it to Bonnell without a dram of remorse. That was the way the man operated.

But, on a personal level, he liked Joe. And Joe liked Rusty. "I apologize for not calling you this weekend, Rusty. The accident happened Saturday morning." Christy filled in the details.

"Well, you're in a fine fix, aren't you?" Rusty sighed. "Keep me closely informed, Christy. You know my position, and I can't change company policy for Joe any more than I could change it for anyone else."

"I understand." It wasn't a lie. She might not like it, but she did understand.

Christy put the receiver down, noticed listlessly that it was sprinkling rain again, then put her head down on her desk and wept. The situation just kept getting worse and worse, and how was she going to hold everything together? She was an accountant, not a logging manager. She remembered Vincent Bonnell's admonition to call him if she hit a snag, but crying on his shoulder would only make her look like a fool. Besides, she didn't trust the man.

Sniffling, she raised her head, found a tissue and blew her nose. She had knocked on Stubb's door until her knuckles hurt, but Stubb hadn't answered. Either he really wasn't home or he was too sick to come to the door. She'd racked her brain for a way to find out which it was all the way from his house to the office, and had come up with only one: call the sheriff.

But, Lord, she hated to involve the law. Stubb and a few of Joe's other employees lived just on the fringes of the law, anyway, and inviting the sheriff to intrude wouldn't exactly make her popular. Especially if Stubb was merely off somewhere on a bender.

The phone rang again, someone asking how Joe was. Within the next half hour Christy answered two more such calls. She turned on the computer and tried to get some work done, but she couldn't concentrate on numbers when her mind was in such turmoil.

Finally she got up and paced. It was another fruitless activity, but she simply couldn't sit still. Wandering into Joe's office, she straightened the items on his desktop, which was always untidy.

Joe had several framed photographs, one of Laura and one of Christy as a teenager. Christy picked up the one of herself and studied it. Years of memories brought tears to her eyes. Poor Joe. He'd always been so good to her, and to her mother. Laura loved him with every fiber of her gentle soul, and she, Christy, loved him, too.

She couldn't give up. These first few days were bound to be the most difficult. The men had to adjust to Joe's absence, and so did she.

When the phone rang again, Christy was positive it was just another well-wisher, so she was startled to hear an operator say, "Would you accept a collect call from a Mr. Stubb Brannigan?"

"Yes! Yes, of course. Stubb? Where are you?"

"I'm in Missoula, Montana, Christy." She heard a feeble laugh. "I don't know what happened, but I woke up in a boxcar."

"A boxcar! My Lord, how would you get into a boxcar without knowing it?"

"Well, I was pretty drunk Saturday night, and I kind of remember a bunch of Bonnell men sneaking around. I don't know for sure, but I think they had something to do with it. Anyway, I don't have any money. Could you wire me enough dough to get home on?"

Three

The most consuming fury of Christy's life made her almost sick to her stomach. She could picture exactly what had happened to Stubb. Bonnell and his unscrupulous crew *knew* Stubb was the only Morrison employee even remotely capable of superintending Joe's operation, and Stubb's unplanned trip was a delaying tactic, a dirty trick to make things even tougher for her! Bonnell wanted Joe's contract, and all of his phony sincerity was nothing but a disgusting joke. "I'll take care of it immediately, Stubb."

"Just send it to Western Union in Missoula. I'll wait there for it. And, Christy, thanks. I won't forget this."

"Hurry home, Stubb." It flashed through Christy's mind that Stubb didn't know about Joe's accident, but she was so worked up, and a fleeting image of herself explaining the situation to Stubb in person the second he got back seemed logical. Putting the phone down, she raced back to her own desk for a company check and her purse. Then she dashed out of the office and into the rain to Joe's pickup.

She made a quick stop at the bank to get some cash, drove to the bus station, which also maintained a small Western Union counter, and took care of the wire.

Back in the pickup again, she drove with her jaw tightly clenched. Bonnell's chowderheaded crew members had gone too far this time. Forgetting all about the indignity of anger, which she had condemned only yesterday, Christy parked in front of the Bonnell Logging Company's office, then marched through the front door.

Myrna Cartwright, whom Christy knew from church, greeted her with obvious surprise. "Why, hello, Christy."

"Hello, Myrna. Is Mr. Bonnell here?" She knew he was. His pickup was parked at the side of the building.

Myrna got up from her desk. "I'll tell him you want to see him. I heard about Joe. I'm terribly sorry."

"Thank you."

While she waited Christy glared at Bonnell's office. She wanted to break something, to do something to destroy the man's peace. Wouldn't he be shocked if she smashed that ugly lamp? Or that ghastly green ashtray?

That's what she wanted to do, shock him. Or, better yet, *sock* him. The smug, smooth-talking, lying jerk!

"Go on in, Christy." Myrna was returning to her desk and Vince was standing in a doorway. It suddenly occurred to Christy that as personally satisfying as throwing a temper tantrum right here and now would be, it would be much better to carry on this little discussion in private.

Her voice dripped icicles. "I need to talk to you."

Myrna's left eyebrow went up. "Would you like me to leave, Vince?"

Vince's eyes narrowed on Christy Allen. If she wasn't on the verge of exploding, he'd better have his eyesight checked. "No, we'll take a ride." He walked to the front door and opened it. Christy darted past him, but when she headed for Joe's pickup, Vince called out, "I'll drive."

Reversing directions, she strode to Vince's truck. He opened the passenger door and waited for her to climb in and settle on the seat before closing it. Then he walked around the truck and got in. Christy stared straight ahead. She was steaming mad, furious, and while everything that was going on wasn't this man's fault, the reason for her fury was!

Vince started the truck. "It's raining again," he commented, as though Christy couldn't see that for herself.

She didn't answer. She didn't want to make any kind of small talk or even be nice to this . . . this person!

Shooting her a questioning look, Vince shrugged and pulled the pickup out of the parking area and onto the street. "Anywhere in particular you'd like to go?"

Christy turned in the seat. "Just pull over. This won't take long."

Vince briefly scanned the curb parking. There were empty spaces, but they were also close to being in the center of town. He couldn't guess why Christy was all puffed up and stiff with anger, but he had a feeling he was going to find out. Which puzzled him, because why would she come to him to let off that steam? "Look, I know you've been under a lot of pressure the last few days, but—"

"You, Mr. Vincent *Bull* Bonnell, are the biggest jerk to ever come down the pike!"

"What?" Vince grinned, then looked at her and laughed. "Where'd you hear that old nickname?"

"This isn't funny! But then with your twisted sense of right or wrong or anything else, you're probably having yourself a real big laugh. I have never met anyone so low, so despicable, so sneaky, so conniving, so—"

"Hey, hey, aren't you getting just a bit carried away?" Vince's smile evolved into a perplexed frown. And he did pull over, although they were halfway out of town now and few people were in the vicinity. He left the engine running because the heater was just beginning to warm up and the air was chilly from the rain. Facing Christy, he asked, "Now, what's this all about?"

"As if you didn't know," she sneered. "All the time I was talking about Stubb, you knew. You rat! You...you stinker!"

Vince grabbed her by the upper arms. "Cool it!" He'd never been around anyone so worked up who hadn't resorted to vulgarity, and Christy's name-calling was really pretty funny. But he couldn't doubt the degree of her anger.

Nor could he doubt the impact she was having on him. How had they lived in the same town for so many years without him noticing her as a woman? Damn, she was sexy!

She probably needed some loving. As far as he knew, she hadn't had a real boyfriend since she'd moved back to Rock Falls, and if there was anything that could make a woman waspish, it was the lack of loving.

He decided to volunteer for the job and brought her forward without any warning. Christy gasped as she realized what he was doing, but that was all she had time for before his mouth covered hers.

"Hmmph!" she shrieked, her big effort to lay him low verbally muffled by Bonnell's lips. And the kiss was thorough...and possessive...and it went on and on. She wriggled and squirmed, but she might as well not have wasted the energy for all the good she did.

Her brain heaped horrible methods of vengeance on him and even approached some much stronger language than *rat* and *stinker*.

And then she became aware of other thoughts, traitorous and insane as they were. His body had to be made of iron, but if it was, it was warm and very vital iron. He was wearing a red-and-blue plaid flannel shirt, and beneath it beat a strong and fearless heart. He was so male, so completely, stunningly male. He smelled like the outdoors and of something subtly spicy.

Oh, dear God, had she ever really, truly been kissed before? Like this? By a big, big man with arms of steel and lips like hot satin?

She couldn't breathe, from both the anger this had started with and the crazy spinning of her insides. Oh, she knew what that spiraling heat in her belly was. A thirty-year-old woman wasn't a kid, and she'd experienced sexual passion before. But this! This implosion of feelings, this crushing, bone-jarring desire... how could she feel such things for a man like Bonnell?

Vince felt something akin to elasticity in her body, and his pulse went wild because he took it as response. His mouth softened, gentled, and he did what he'd been wanting to do since Saturday—gather up a handful of her incredible hair. It was damp and silky and caressing to his hand.

"Christy," he hoarsely whispered against her lips. "Oh, baby. I didn't expect..."

She tore her mouth free. But she needed air so badly that she gulped in a big breath before she said anything, and then when she spoke, it came out sounding like a hiss. "You... you... how dare you!"

Vince sensed her rising hand, her fingernails aimed for his face. He caught both of her hands. "Wait a minute. Honey, you kissed me back!"

"Like hell I did! Let go of me."

They stared into each other's eyes, Christy's narrowed and dark green with fury, Vince's narrowed and speculative. He wasn't breathing very easily. The kiss had knocked him for a loop. She was one special lady, but he suspected she would rather die than admit she had liked that kiss.

"All right, all right. Calm down. That was probably a stupid move, but I did it without thinking."

"*Probably* stupid? I can't believe your gall! I don't happen to enjoy being mauled!"

"I didn't maul you," Vince groaned disgustedly. "If I let go of your hands, will you calm down and tell me what the hell got you so fighting mad?"

Staring Bonnell down took an inordinate amount of strength, and Christy suddenly lost hers. Her fight, too. All at once she felt a lot more like crying than she did fighting.

She was in the biggest mess of her life, the biggest mess of Joe's life, and she was so wretchedly helpless. Everywhere she turned there was another hurdle, another problem.

The tears couldn't be held back, and they began to spill over her bottom lashes and drip down her cheeks. "Aw, hell," Vince muttered, and released her hands to draw her head against his chest. "What's the matter? I know things look bleak right now, but I told you I'd help wherever I could. Why are you so mad at me?"

Christy only let one shuddering sob escape. She still had *some* pride left, and crying on Bonnell's broad chest was the most humiliating experience of her life. "Don't play games with me," she said dully.

He tipped her chin to see her face. "I already apologized for that pass."

"I'm not talking about that!" Angry again, Christy sat up and away from him. "It's Stubb."

"Oh, yeah, you did mention Stubb. What about him?"

"He's in Missoula, Montana, as if you didn't know!"

"In Missoula! Now, how would I know he went to Missoula?"

"He went to Missoula in a boxcar!"

"A what?"

"Your men put him in it Saturday night when he was dead drunk!"

It took a second, but then the whole thing hit Vince hard. Stubb Brannigan rode a boxcar to Missoula? Drunk as a skunk? Vince started to laugh, and he couldn't stop. That was the funniest thing he'd heard of in he couldn't remember when. He could see a picture of Stubb waking up with a head the size of a barrel and wondering where in hell he was, then figuring out he was in a boxcar in Missoula, Montana.

Vince roared while Christy stewed. She fidgeted, and he still laughed. She inundated him with dirty looks, and he kept right on whooping.

"I'm certainly glad you're getting such a bang out of this," she finally said peevishly.

Vince wiped his eyes. He hadn't had such a genuinely good laugh in years. In fact, the picture of Stubb waking up in a boxcar in Missoula kept tickling him, and he laughed some more. Finally he began to regain control. "I've never heard anything so funny in my life."

"I'm glad I'm so amusing."

Shaking his head, Vince surrendered to one more bout of laughter. Then he cleared his throat. "You're amusing, honey, but not nearly as funny as Stubb." It wasn't exactly the best thing he could have said, he realized when Christy suddenly grabbed for the door handle. "Just a minute! Where do you think you're going?" he yelled, catching her just a second before she slid to the ground.

"I'm tired of this stupid conversation," she cried. "Let go of me, you . . . you bully!"

"Don't be silly. It's a long walk back to my office and it's pouring out. I'll drive you back. Settle down."

She really had no tremendous urge to get soaked to the skin, although if he didn't stop his irritating laughter and snide remarks, she *would* walk back.

With the door closed again Vince looked at her. One thing was dead certain: he was getting off on the wrong foot with Christy Allen. And that idea didn't set right. Not that he was in desperate need of female companionship. Rock Falls had all kinds of available women, and he was never lonesome if he didn't want to be.

But Christy was different. Very different. She was intelligent and exciting, and she reached something in Vince Bonnell that he hadn't even known he possessed. Something tender and even a little boyish. And God knows he had given up his boyhood a long, long time ago.

Now life consisted of hard work, adult worries and only an occasional deviation from routine. His business was demanding, which he wasn't complaining about. He loved the logging business, even with all of its seasonal ups and downs and its never-ending fluctuations every time the government came up with another regulation, or the economy dipped, or some environmentalist discovered another endangered species of animal or bird in the woods. How many times had he read a report on housing starts in the country taking a drop and known that somehow, someway, even if the biggest drop was in the east, he was going to feel its repercussion?

Well, every logger in the business had the same problems. It took tough, thick-skinned people to battle weather, equipment and bureaucracy on a daily basis, month after month, year after year. Sure, loggers played hard, and some of them, like Stubb, drank too much. But they worked like Trojans and earned every penny of their pay.

Vince had never felt it necessary to apologize to anyone for either himself or his preferences. He wasn't overly educated, having barely made it through high school. But he was a top-notch logger, and he would put his knowledge and expertise up against any man's. He was rawhide tough, and he knew that as fact, not boast.

But this slip of a woman, this tiny little thing with the teary gray-green eyes and more hair than any one woman should be blessed with, had made him recognize a spot of softness deep inside of himself, one that he'd never suspected was there. Was that why he'd been trying to help her? The impulse had started out because of Joe, but it was Christy who was egging him on, not Joe.

He was suddenly horribly, unfamiliarly uncomfortable. Grabbing Christy and kissing her the way he'd done was the act of a cretin. What the hell had gotten into him?

"Christy, I'm sorry."

"You should be." She paused. "I thought you were going to take me back to my pickup."

"I am. I *will*. Only, I want you to understand that I don't usually grab women I hardly know. Or who hardly know me," he added lamely.

Christy turned her head to give him a startled look. "I'm talking about what your men did to Stubb, *not* that pass. Which, of course, was certainly uncalled for. But I have a lot more important things on my mind than a kiss right now.''

Which was the God's truth. She would think about Bonnell's unmitigated gall later... and maybe even relive her strange and alarming response to the man. It needed looking into, she felt, but not now. Not when she was sick with worry over events she honestly didn't know how to deal with.

Vince saw the worry on her face and the turmoil in her eyes, and his heart turned over. He'd told her to come to him for help, and when she did, he'd behaved like an idiot. Sure, she'd been madder than a wet hen, but why wouldn't she be? It wasn't Morrison men who had crammed old Stubb into a boxcar headed for Montana.

Vince actually had to clench his jaw to keep from laughing again. It *was* funny, even if it was also serious. He rubbed his mouth, willing the urge to pass. ''Look, I'll have a talk with my men, okay?''

Sighing dejectedly, Christy leaned her head back. ''What good would it do? They'd probably all crack up just like you did.''

''I know one thing, Christy. They didn't do it with the intention of hurting anyone. It was a joke. Hell, Stubb's the biggest jokester in town.''

Christy raised her head. ''Stubb is?''

''He is with... well, I guess you'd call it the drinking crowd. If he's not pulling a fast one, someone else is. One time he and Sonny Paulson took Mac Rogers five miles out of town, stole his pants and let him walk back in his skivvies.''

''Oh, great,'' Christy drawled dryly. ''Well, apparently those delightful stories ordinarily elude me. Unfortunately I'm right in the middle of all that hilarity right now. I'm sorry I bothered you. I can see now that you can't control your crew any more than I can control Morrison employees.''

"You can only control your crew during working hours, Christy. Their free time is their own, and most of the loggers around here are pretty substantial citizens, men with families."

"That's why places like the Way Inn do such a thriving business," she retorted, again dryly.

"Don't be bitter, Christy."

"I'm not bitter, but I am a little overwhelmed right now."

"I know you are. Have you thought about what I suggested?"

Christy released an exasperated breath. "It's out of the question. I can't imagine why you think I could handle a logging crew."

"Because you know the business."

"Oh, sure. I went up to the logging site this morning and almost had a coronary over an overturned truck and a road full of logs. Some expert I am!"

"What happened?"

Christy explained, wondering in the back of her mind why she was telling this man anything. Maybe she had to talk to someone, she told herself, even if he was the one person in Rock Falls she shouldn't be talking to.

"Well, that's a costly accident, all right. But did you stop to think that if you'd been there it might not have happened?"

"How on earth would I have made a difference?"

"All I know is that a ship runs a whole lot smoother with a good captain at its helm. Think about it." Vince reached for the gearshift. "By the way, you can bother me anytime you want to."

She sent him a questioning look, which he was glad to clear up. "You apologized for bothering me, and I just said for you to bother me anytime you want to."

Why was it that when she was with Bonnell she almost believed what he said, and then when she was alone she saw him as some kind of clever manipulator? Did he want Joe's contract or didn't he? Would he stoop so low as to be nice to her in person and then scheme behind her back?

Just how far did Joe trust Vince Bonnell? If she could only talk to Joe...

That was impossible, and there was no point in thinking along those lines. Joe wouldn't be alert enough to converse intelligently about anything for days, and even then, disturbing subjects would only add to the frustration Christy knew he would be feeling.

Joe was an active, purely physical man. Once he woke up enough to understand how long he was going to be laid up, he was going to be one unhappy individual. Laura would be his best medicine. Her gentleness had always seemed to soothe her roaring lion of a husband, and it would be Laura who would keep Joe calm.

No, she couldn't go to Joe, Christy acknowledged wearily. Not with worries, not with complaints, certainly not with references to Bonnell's intrusion into Morrison affairs. She would put on an impassive face whenever she saw Joe; it was the only humane thing to do.

The drive back to his office took only a few minutes. Vince parked the truck and turned off the engine. He wanted to ask Christy out for supper and glanced at her speculatively. She no doubt called the evening meal dinner. She was a classy, educated lady, and he was a rough-hewn lumberjack. The differences between them suddenly seemed monumental, something he personally had never run into with a woman before.

He cleared his throat with unusual nervousness. "I was thinking. How about...well, you have to eat, anyway. How about eating with me tonight?"

Why, he was asking for a date! Christy stared at him, trying to read the expression in his eyes. And what marvelous eyes they were, reminding her of dark gray velvet. Except, of course, they weren't completely gray. She was positive Bonnell's eyes contained flecks of black and gold. She would know for sure if she was a little closer to him, which would be a foolish move for her to make. After that kiss any kind of personal overture would be foolish. And she didn't trust him.

As for eating with him tonight, that would be pure folly and uncomfortable, besides. What did they have to talk about? Stubb? Their companies' respective logging contracts? The fact that Joe's accident had put Bonnell in the catbird's seat with Rennard Lumber Company?

Or maybe she could tell him that she had once known a man very much like him, a brash, handsome, know-everything guy who had stomped all over her heart.

The idea was ludicrous, of course. She would tell Vince Bonnell no such private information about herself, although it had been the first thing she had thought of the day he had appeared at the hospital, all confidence and swagger.

Christy didn't have to hedge, which she was glad to rely on: she truly couldn't spare the time. "I'll be eating dinner with my mother at the hospital. I've got work at the office that I can't delay doing any longer, and once that's finished I have to go and see Joe."

Somehow Vince had known she would refuse, but foresight didn't relieve the disappointment he felt. He really wasn't accustomed to being turned down, either, which in itself pricked his ego.

"Maybe some other time," he mumbled, a little embarrassed that he'd even thought she might agree. *Hoped* she would.

Christy reached for the door handle. "I've got to get going." She didn't know if she should thank him for this meeting or leave without mentioning it. It had accomplished nothing other than giving him a good laugh, after all.

He was a puzzling, enigmatic man, and it was best to stay away from him. She would think twice before seeking him out again, no matter how upset or accusing she became. Somehow she would get through this, and so would Joe and her mother. And they would do it without Vincent Bonnell, too.

"Goodbye." Christy jumped out of the truck, with Vince getting out on the driver's side. He stood in the rain, his gaze on her as she walked to Joe's pickup. Then he watched it driving away with a strange, incomprehensible emptiness.

What the heck was going on with him? Was he falling for Christy Allen?

With his forehead deeply creased by a frown, Vince turned and walked to the front door of his office building.

Laura was all smiles. "He was awake several times today."

Christy hugged her mother. "Oh, I'm so glad, Mom."

They were in Joe's room, speaking in hushed tones. "Dr. Martin told me that he plans to have Joe moved out of Intensive Care in the morning."

That was very good news, the first step in Joe's long road to recovery. "Wonderful."

"Laura?"

Both women moved to the bed. "I'm here, dear," Laura murmured softly, taking Joe's unbandaged left hand. "Christy's here, too."

"Hello, Joe. How are you feeling?"

Joe's pale blue eyes attempted to focus on his stepdaughter. "Like a tree fell on me."

Christy smiled. It was only a very small joke, but a good sign that Joe was progressing. "You took a bad spill."

Joe's pale blue eyes closed for a few seconds, then opened again. "How're things going, Christy?"

She knew he was talking about the business. "Things are going just fine," she lied. "I don't want you worrying about a thing, do you hear?"

"You're a good girl," Joe whispered, and his eyes closed again.

After a moment Christy and Laura tiptoed away from the bed and out to the corridor. "He's got a...a contraption on him that administers a steady flow of some kind of sedative. Dr. Martin explained it to me, but I really don't understand how it works. Anyway, Joe's pretty heavily sedated and not in any real pain," Laura said with a grateful sigh.

"He's getting very good care," Christy concurred. "Mom, you must be tired of hospital food. Let's run down to Mabel's and have a decent meal."

Laura glanced at the door to Joe's room, then nodded. "All right. On the way out I'll tell the floor nurse where we'll be."

Mabel's Café served as close to home-cooked food as a restaurant could, and they ordered and ate while Laura related her day at Joe's bedside in great detail. Christy listened and made appropriate comments, but her thoughts kept drifting to her own day.

Vince's kiss was etched in her soul. It seemed incredible now that she hadn't become more emotional about it at the time. Oh, she'd felt plenty of emotion, too much for her own peace of mind, actually. But she'd been so indignant, so full of righteous anger over Stubb's maltreatment, and the kiss had taken her by surprise.

It would stay with her for a long time. She wasn't kissed enough anymore to forget one, in any case. But those few moments in Vince's arms had been earthshaking. And she was beginning to realize just how earthshaking.

Christy put her fork down, unable to eat another bite. She sipped from her glass of water while Laura talked about one thing and she worried about another. The abbreviated conversation with Stubb was starting to gnaw at her. She had sent him enough money for a plane ticket, so even with the last lap of the trip encompassing a bus ride from Portland to Rock Falls, Stubb should be back no later than this evening.

But she didn't know for sure, did she? There had been nothing definite said about time and necessity.

She should have informed Stubb, very distinctly, of Joe's accident and how badly he was needed at the logging site.

What if he took his time coming back? What if he dawdled and fooled around in Montana for a while? He had some money now, and what if he started drinking again?

If only she had explained the situation on the phone. Instead she had gotten angry at Bonnell and his moronic logging crew and common sense had flown right out the window. Some businesswoman she was! Joe was depending on her, Laura was depending on her, and she, herself, knew better than either Joe or Laura just how crucial her role in the operation was right now. And yet she had let emotion override sensibility.

She had a lot to learn about running a business, obviously.

There were things to do yet tonight. She had to talk to Clem, for one. Until Stubb got back she *had* to lean on Clem, like it or not. Poor Clem. He might have the know-how, but he had absolutely no desire to shoulder the responsibility. She could only force Clem to be acting foreman for a brief, *very* brief, period of time.

Christy dropped Laura back at the hospital and then drove home. It was no longer raining, but darkness was falling early because of the heavy, overhanging clouds.

It occurred to her, as she unlocked the front door of her house and reached down to pet Muffin, that she was in a day-by-day situation. What would tomorrow bring? And the next day?

Sighing, Christy fed and watered Muffin, then went to the telephone. She would try Stubb's number, then call Clem. Maybe Stubb was back and she would have good news for Clem.

After looking up Stubb Brannigan's telephone number, she dialed it with a prayer in her heart.

Four

Stubb didn't answer his phone, and maybe just as bad, neither did Clem answer his. What had Joe done when he'd needed to talk to one of his men and couldn't readily reach him?

Christy knew the answer to that question before it even completely formed in her mind: Joe went looking. Nothing daunted Joe, certainly not a dark and rainy night. But she wasn't Joe, and doing things his way wasn't going to be easy.

Going to the living room window, Christy wrapped her arms around herself and gazed out. The light on her gatepost seemed to be wavering, all dim and watery at the end of the walk. For the first time since Christy had returned to Rock Falls she regretted her rather solitary life-style. A really close friend would be a comfort right now, someone who would listen and commiserate. She had friends, of course, but no one she could turn to with a pack of troubles.

That status was all her own doing. Her years away from Rock Falls had put her out of touch with school chums, and when she moved back, she had learned that her closest pals had left the area. Since, she'd been content with very little social life, and one didn't make close friends in a town this size by avoiding events that almost everyone else enjoyed.

Christy believed she understood herself very well. The thrilling excitement and then the heartbreaking demise of the one major romance in her life had immeasurably affected her. Up until now she hadn't thought there was anything missing from her quiet way of life, but there were definitely doubts plaguing her tonight. So... what was the missing piece—a friend to confide in?

Or a man who didn't ask before he kissed?

Christy frowned. The reason she had felt so much when Bonnell kissed her was because it had been so long since any man had kissed her. That was all there was to it.

Actually, she should be offended. Examining her own reactions, however, Christy knew that echoes of that kiss were still alive in her system. Today Vince Bonnell had very effectively reminded her that she was a woman and most certainly that he was a man. What was more, there seemed to be some kind of crazy chemistry between them.

Christy sighed dismally. That's all she needed right now, a personal relationship with a man she shouldn't even be speaking to. Bonnell would snap up Joe's contract in a minute, given the opportunity, and that was what she should be concerned about, not that the man's kiss had been sinfully delicious.

Or maybe she should rearrange adjectives. Wasn't deliciously sinful a more appropriate description of Bonnell's overwhelming sex appeal?

Sinful was right on the money, Christy decided. At least that kiss was making her *think* about sin, and making it look pretty darn tempting, too.

Well, standing around and dissecting Vince Bonnell was getting her nowhere. She had to find out if Stubb had returned to town, or if he was lost somewhere between Oregon and Montana.

Leaving the window, Christy tried Stubb's number again, broke the unanswered connection after five rings and dialed Clem's number. She allowed five rings on that call, too, then impatiently dropped the receiver back into its cradle. It was imperative that she talk to Clem tonight. For one thing, Stubb or no Stubb, it was absolutely crucial that the Morrison crew deliver some logs to the sawmill tomorrow.

And, heaven help her, if Clem couldn't promise log deliveries, she was going to have to go out to that logging site in the morning and try to do something about it. She couldn't just sit by and watch Joe's contract fly away. Maybe candor would get the men more receptive to organizing themselves. If they truly understood how dire things were...

But that wasn't her best course, either. Christy knew that Joe didn't discuss the business end of his operation with his crew. He wouldn't appreciate her reciting the due dates of bank loans nor the rigid terms of his logging contract to anyone, least of all his employees.

She was in a pickle, any way she looked at it. Disheartened, Christy got her jacket and purse and left the house.

A half hour later Christy spied Clem's red Wagoneer in the High-Ridge Café's parking lot. Relief ran through her, and she quickly pulled off the road and parked as close to the building as she could get. The drizzle dampened her hair on the way in, but then, just inside the door, she saw Clem in a booth, calmly reading the newspaper and sipping from a coffee mug.

With the dinner hour long past, the café was nearly empty. Clem looked up as Christy approached. ''Hello,'' he said with a wariness that alerted Christy to probable difficulties ahead.

Putting on a friendly smile, she slid into the vacant side of the booth. "I was hoping you would contact me at the end of the workday, Clem."

"I stopped by the office, but you weren't there."

He had made only one attempt to reach her, but she couldn't chide him for it. A woman in her position didn't scold a man like Clem Molinski.

A waitress called from behind the counter. "Do you want a menu, Christy?"

"Nothing, Molly, thanks." Christy turned back to Clem, vowing to be tactful. "I don't think you realize how important you are to the operation right now, Clem."

The old man looked stubbornly opposed to this conversation. "Never wanted to be important."

Christy's voice gentled. "Was acting as foreman today really so terrible?"

Clem folded his newspaper and scowled across the table. "I ain't cut out to tell other people what to do. Never was, never will be. I do my job and collect my pay. Been doing it for almost fifty years."

"But you couldn't do your job today, Clem. There was only one truck loaded out with logs today, and it never made it down the mountain. So what did you do all day? What did the other men do?"

"The sawyers worked."

"But downed trees lying in the woods don't put bread on the table. Clem, none of us will get one penny until those logs are delivered to the mill."

"You have to pay the sawyers no matter what," Clem mumbled.

That was true, but Christy didn't feel much like discussing common payroll practices at the moment. "My point is," she said a little more aggressively, "without deliveries there won't be any money to pay anyone with. Clem, you've worked in the logging industry all your life and you've been with Joe for years. You know exactly how he runs his operation. What's so difficult about overseeing it?'' She leaned forward. ''I'll pay you more money,'' she pleaded.

Clem turned his head and stared off across the café. When he looked at her again, his expression was more lenient. ''Christy, it ain't the money. Some of us are leaders and some of us ain't. There ain't a man in Joe's crew who's not a danged good worker, but without Joe we're all like...like a band without a guy waving a baton at 'em. Do you understand what I'm trying to say? Without Joe the operation's out of sync.''

It wasn't anything she didn't already know. In fact, Clem was arguing her very side in this going-nowhere conversation.

''Have you heard anything from Stubb?'' Clem asked. ''Old Stubb could straighten everything out almost as good as Joe.''

''I'm still looking for him,'' Christy replied, deciding to keep Stubb's misadventure to herself. It would get around soon enough, and when it did, God only knew what form of retaliation the Morrison crew would wreak on Bonnell's men. ''In your opinion, Clem, will there be log deliveries tomorrow?''

''Should be.''

His noncommittal reply finished deflating Christy. She got up slowly. ''All right, Clem, I'll stop badgering you. Just do the best you can tomorrow, all right?''

''That's all anyone can do.''

He wasn't about to make excuses for his less-than-cooperative attitude, which really didn't surprise Christy. Men like Clem Molinski apologized to no one for anything, and certainly not because of their work ethics. Maybe the hard work they did made them harder men.

''Good night, Clem,'' she said quietly, and walked to the door. Outside, she took a deep breath of the moist, fresh air. She might as well face it. Without Stubb she was also without a paddle and up the proverbial creek. Clem's desultory supervision was little better than none, and she couldn't force the stubborn old logger to put more effort into something he had no taste for.

Christy drove past Stubb's house again, which was still dark and obviously uninhabited. The man was somewhere in Montana, probably having a great old time on the money she'd wired to bring him home. She slapped the steering wheel in frustration and muttered a word she never used.

Instead of going home, Christy drove to the office. Inside, she switched on every light, took off her jacket and sat at her desk. What, precisely, were her options?

Ever organized, Christy got out a pad and pen and wrote "number one" on the first line. But staring at her own neat handwriting didn't suddenly give her any brilliant ideas and her few options really didn't have to be spelled out. She could and would contact the State Employment Service and let them know she was in desperate need of a logging supervisor, she could continue to coax Clem, which seemed utterly futile, or she could...

No, she couldn't consider Bonnell's suggestion! Too agitated to sit still, Christy threw down the pen and got up. Shoving her hands into the side pockets of her slacks, she walked around the silent office and worried. That was what she was best at, she decided disgustedly, worry. But she couldn't see herself up at that logging site issuing orders to men who were twice her size and had few qualms about telling anyone who got in their way to go to hell.

Not that any of the crew had ever treated her disrespectfully. They came into the office on occasion, and not one of them had ever given her so much as an out-of-the-way look. Like Bonnell had said, most of the area's loggers were family men and only interested in making a decent living. In all fairness only a minority hung out at places like the Way Inn.

Dear Lord, what was she going to do? Her deepest concern about attempting to ramrod the logging operation wasn't with the men; it was with her own inability! Her worry was becoming a prayer, she realized, encompassing Joe, her mother, the business and herself.

A sudden knock at the door nearly scared Christy to death. Thankful that she had thought to lock it when she came in, she called out, "Who is it?"

"Vince Bonnell. What are you doing here at this time of night? Are you all right?"

"Oh, good grief," Christy muttered. She unlocked the dead bolt and opened the door. "I'm just fine. What are you doing here?"

Vince came in and blatantly looked around, as if expecting to see some threat lurking in the shadows. "I was driving past and saw the lights."

For a moment his back was to Christy, and she found herself marveling at the breadth of Bonnell's shoulders. His height was magnificent and so was his head of thick, dark hair. He was an uncommonly attractive man, whether she liked admitting it or not.

He turned around with a skeptically raised eyebrow. "Working late?"

She almost retorted, "*Worrying* late," but stopped herself in time. A firmly stated "Yes" was the lie that came out of her mouth. "I don't seem to be getting much done during the day," she added, simply because she never had been a very convincing liar and sensed that Bonnell didn't believe her.

Vince pointedly glanced at the lifeless computer on her desk. "I was just getting ready to leave," Christy said defensively. She hated lies for this very reason. One always led to another.

"Christy, I drove by here not more than a half hour ago and the place was dark."

Embarrassment colored her cheeks. Getting caught was only a liar's just punishment, but this man had no right to question her activities. "Are you patrolling the area for a specific reason?" she asked sharply.

He grinned impudently, taking her resentful criticism as funny. "I'm not patrolling, sweetheart. But neither are you working." His smile faded. "You were in here worrying, weren't you?"

Christy threw up her hands. "Just who pronounced you my protector, Bonnell? Or maybe you've decided to take care of *all* of the Morrison family. This is pretty darn peculiar, don't you think?"

He stared for a long moment. "Yes, I guess it is. Would you rather I minded my own business?"

Again that deflated sensation struck Christy, a feeling very similar, she supposed, to wind-billowed sails suddenly losing a sea breeze. Despising the very thought of helplessness was a poor defense against the debilitating feeling, and as lamentable as the situation was, Vince Bonnell was the only person in Rock Falls who seemed to care if she sank or swam.

Christy felt herself drawn to his concern, genuine or not. In fact, repugnant as the possibility was, it would be a very simple matter to get totally female right now and let a few tears fall.

Vince saw her tough facade beginning to crumble and also her attempt to conceal it. She was a gutsy little thing, but determination alone wasn't going to solve her problems. "Look," he said softly, "I only want to help. Tell me where you're at. Did Stubb get back?"

Swallowing the lump of tears in her throat, Christy shook her head. "Not yet. I...I made a mistake with Stubb. When he called from Montana, he needed money to get home on. I wired it immediately, but I was so worked up over his story that I didn't tell him about Joe's accident, or that it was crucial he get back as fast as possible."

Vince got the picture. Unaware of the situation in Rock Falls, Stubb was probably taking his sweet time coming home. He could be enjoying himself at any given point between Rock Falls, Oregon, and Missoula, Montana. "I don't suppose you have any idea where you might reach him."

"None."

"Well, he'll show up sooner or later."

"Yes, I'm sure he will." Christy was grateful that Vince hadn't made some cutting remark about her ineptitude. He very well could have when it was so obvious that she had gotten angry at his men's shenanigans rather than clarify the situation for Stubb.

Vince sat on the corner of her desk. "Did your crew clear the road of that spilled load of logs?"

"I think so. I saw Clem a few minutes ago at the Hi-Ridge, and—" Christy angrily raked a handful of hair back from her face as she realized she hadn't asked Clem if the road had been cleared. Actually, she'd merely assumed this morning that it would be and let it go at that. My Lord, the details Joe juggled were incredible! How had she worked in this office for five years and not realized the complexity of his duties?

Glumly she sank onto a chair and stared at Vince, who was staring back with an unreadable expression. "I can't do it," she said dully. "I'm a bookkeeper, not a manager. There's a lot more to the logging business than cutting and hauling logs to the mill. Just keeping track of the crew is a full-time job."

Vince laughed softly. "It's not usually this bad. Joe will tell you that himself when he can."

"I remember him rounding up one man or another many times," Christy rebutted.

"Oh, sure, it happens. Something comes up and you have to get hold of a particular man outside of working hours. But normally the men go to work in the morning, do their job and go home at quitting time."

"It's that 'doing their job' bit that's got me stymied," Christy admitted grimly. "Clem said it tonight. Without Joe the operation's out of sync."

"And it probably will be until someone takes hold of it. What about Clem? He's an old hand. Maybe he would—" Vince stopped when he saw the look on Christy's face. "You've already tried Clem, right?"

Getting to her feet, Christy walked a circle around the room, giving Bonnell a wide berth. She was talking too much, detailing her weak position to the only man in town who could benefit from it. The next thing out of her mouth was apt to be a reference to that five-figure bank loan due in two weeks, and that was something Joe would never forgive.

On top of all that, saying right out that she couldn't do the job was probably the most spineless, disloyal thing she could ever have done. She *had* to do the job, and whining to Vince Bonnell was disgusting. "I'll figure something out," she said through clenched teeth.

Vince caught on to her abrupt reversal. For a minute or two they'd been on the same wavelength, but she was guarded again now. He watched her pacing, absorbing and enjoying the sight of her small figure moving around the room. That kiss in his truck had stayed with him all day. Her mouth had been sweet and warm, despite very little cooperation on her part, and the feel of her body was still on his hands.

He cleared his throat. "Christy, what about me going up to your job tomorrow and—"

She whirled. "Absolutely not! Your name already came up, and some of the men would quit—" she snapped her fingers "—that fast if you interfered."

"Interfered? That's not what I'm trying to do, you know."

"That's how Joe's men would see it."

"And you? How do you see it?"

He was attempting to turn this into something personal, she realized with some amazement. That smooth-as-silk quality in his voice was better suited to a bedroom than an office. Her chin rose a fraction. If he was thinking about another kiss, he was in for a rude awakening. "I don't know what to think. Just when did you and Joe become friends?"

Vince grinned. "Maybe I'm not doing this for Joe. Maybe I'm doing it for you."

"For me! You never so much as said hello to me before last Saturday."

An amused shrug lifted Vince's shoulders. "Can't be perfect in everything."

Christy's eyes widened. "Meaning that you are perfect in most things? My, you do have an ego, don't you?"

Lazily Vince uncoiled his long frame and stood up. "I'm not much for apologies, but I'm real sorry about one big oversight. You. How did we keep missing each other? Age? Yeah, that probably had something to do with it. I have to be six or seven years older than you are." He folded his arms across his chest. "You were never married, were you?"

"It's no secret," Christy said, dampening her dry lips. Vince was succeeding in his bid for a personal turn in the conversation; she was being drawn into the scenario, wise or not.

"And you moved back here about four, five years ago."

"You've asked people about me, haven't you?"

"A few questions never hurt anyone."

That opinion sounded debatable to Christy; she wasn't at all sure she liked Vince Bonnell tossing her name around Rock Falls. Some people could get the wrong idea, and her loyalties lay with Joe, no matter how broad Bonnell's shoulders were. Or how appealing his dark gray eyes were becoming.

What had she heard about him and women? Yes, there had been a few women's names linked with his. But he'd never been married, either.

Christy gave her head a sharp shake. Bonnell's love life meant nothing to her! Why would she even be thinking about it? "I would appreciate your not seeking information about me from anyone I know," she said coolly. "This crisis will pass, and when it does and everything gets back to normal, I intend to be able to look Joe in the eye without some kind of guilty hang-up because of you."

"Oh? I make you feel guilty?"

She really wasn't up to a standoff with Vincent Bonnell, but neither could she let him think she was willing to linger here and talk silly. He was flirting, quite obviously hoping for participation. "You know exactly where any guilt I might be feeling lies," she said stiffly.

"The competition between Joe's company and mine?"

He was saying one thing and inferring another. The tone of his voice and the glint in his eyes referred to that kiss as clearly as if he had mentioned it aloud. And Christy wondered about herself and why she felt so female and edgy just because this man had kissed her and insisted on keeping her aware of it.

Vince liked the electricity in the air, and the more he saw of Christy Allen, the better he liked her, too. He was normally a man of few words, but he had the strangest urge to say pretty things to her, soft, flattering references to her cloud of chestnut hair, the arousing depth of her gray-green eyes, the exciting fullness of her bottom lip, romantic things.

"I've got an idea," he said suddenly.

"I'll just bet you do," Christy retorted, then blushed again.

He laughed, freely and with too much enjoyment for Christy's comfort. "Honey, I've got several ideas, but I was referring to the mess you're in. How about you and me going up to Joe's job on Saturday? The crew won't be in the woods, and I can give you some pointers on how to keep things rolling."

His offer stunned Christy. She blinked and wondered why he would take the time to do that for her. On the heels of that conjecture was doubt, and then suspicion, and finally a heated wave of mistrust. "Why would you go out of your way to keep this company going?" she asked bluntly.

To her annoyance he shrugged, as though her question was too trivial to rate any real concern. "How about it? No one would have to know, especially Joe's men." He grinned. "It would be our little secret."

There was that sensual tone again. Sharing a "secret," even one as prosaic as this would be, would alter their relationship, and if she was worried about something personal happening between them, sharing *anything* with this man would be pure stupidity.

"I don't think that's a very good idea," Christy declared, and started around her desk to get her jacket and purse.

"Do you have a better one?"

Even if she had a solid game plan in mind, would it be smart to confide it to the one person who would profit from the demise of Joe's business? Bonnell had wasted no time in barging into Morrison affairs, and while he might be all worked up now at the idea of the two of them sharing a secret, his interference—yes, *interference*—hadn't initially been prompted by a desire to know her better.

He didn't look like a clever, manipulative man. He looked rugged and outdoorsy. Straightforward. Guileless.

She didn't dare trust his exterior appeal; there was too much at stake. Joe had put his life into this business, and right now she was its sole custodian. Maybe she hadn't done a very good job so far, but the shock of it all had been pretty overwhelming. One thing for certain, she had told Bonnell too much about her fears and apprehensions, and that sort of candor had to come to a screeching halt.

Christy slipped into her jacket. "My 'better' idea is merely to keep this business going without your assistance. Joe wouldn't approve of it any more than his men would. I'm not going to sneak around behind anyone's back or…"

"Damn! Christy, you're being very foolish." His outburst startled her, and she stared wide-eyed at the suddenly harder expression on his face. "Why are people so afraid to trust one another? I'm not after Joe's contract, but how can I convince you of that? Joe's in a helluva fix, but let's not forget that his business wouldn't be in jeopardy if he hadn't hung on to control so tightly.

"If something happened to me and I were laid up like Joe is, my foreman would keep the operation running. Joe's just like my dad was, positive that no one else can do his job. Well, let me tell you something about that very dangerous attitude. There's no such thing as being irreplaceable, and you're going to have to prove that very point to Joe.

"Only, you can't and won't do the job in exactly the same way as he does. That's what you've got to accept. Stop worrying about what Joe will think about your methods. If you get the job done, what difference does it make how? And if someone offers to help, take it and don't stop to ask if Joe or his crew or anyone else will like it."

Christy felt very much like a well-chastised child. Bonnell's advice, although grating, was an adult, mature viewpoint. She swallowed nervously, unable to come up with any sort of opposing statement. Her goal was to keep Joe's business intact until he could resume its operation, and she was allowing that silly feud between the two logging companies to influence her judgment.

"Saturday?" she said in a small voice.

Vince nodded. "Unless Stubb gets back. Frankly I'm not all that positive he can do the job. He probably can if he wants to, but that's something you won't know until he shows up."

Picking up her purse, Christy walked to the door. "It's getting late."

Glancing at his watch, Vince agreed. "Time for bed," he commented, giving her a slow grin so full of innuendo that she felt her cheeks getting warm again. Obviously the man was going to keep her fully cognizant of his sex appeal. She only wished she wasn't so prone to blushes with him.

Which was darn strange and irritating, too. When had she become so childishly uncertain of herself that a little flirting unnerved her to the point of an almost constant red face?

Sighing to herself, Christy noticed all of the lights still burning and left the door and turned them off. Vince helped by switching off the lamp on her desk, and then everything was dark and they were both heading out of the office. Stopping to lock the dead bolt, Christy was aware of Bonnell standing very close to her.

She turned with her key ring in her hand. A distant streetlight cast eerie shadows. It wasn't raining now, but puddles gleamed here and there in the parking lot. Bonnell towered over her, making her feel even smaller than she was.

And then he touched her, a brush of calloused fingertips along her cheek. "You just don't know what to make of me, do you?" he asked softly.

She wanted to back away, but some internal force was holding her in place. "No, I don't."

He wanted to kiss her again, to scoop her up in his arms and kiss her breathless. But he stood there and willed himself to be content with the silky texture of her cheek against his fingertips. "Trust me," he said huskily. "Believe that I wouldn't intentionally do anything to hurt you or anyone else, Joe included."

"I . . . I'm trying."

He smiled. "Good. That's a start." Dropping his hand, Vince took her arm to assist her down from the small porch. "If Stubb gets back, let me know. I'll stay in touch, in any case."

She felt rather dazed, she realized as he literally tucked her into the cab of Joe's pickup. The man was very persuasive, very positive, very influencing.

During the drive home, Christy kept glancing at the headlights reflected in her rearview mirror. Vince was seeing that she got home safely.

And, heaven help her, her insides were all mushy and over-heated because of him. Merely because he had touched her in the most casual way possible.

She drew a long, troubled breath. Joe's accident was having some very peculiar side effects. Never in her wildest imagination could she ever have depicted herself and Vince Bonnell becoming friendly.

And friendship wasn't all he wanted from her, either, which presented another disturbing array of speculation. She wasn't a raving beauty and had a few brains, two factors that dramatically distanced her from the type of woman Bonnell normally favored.

She wouldn't be used, Christy determined with a tear glistening in the corner of her eye. Trust him? How could she? There were too many loose ends dangling every which way for her to put her complete trust in Vince.

But she only thought that distinctly when she was by herself. When she was with Vince, nothing seemed very cut and dried.

Five

Rusty Parnell was on the phone at three the following afternoon. "Christy, the mill received four loads of logs today."

She winced. Four loads, when a normal workday produced a dozen and a good day reached fifteen, sixteen loads. "There will be more tomorrow, Rusty."

"I sure hope so. How's Joe?"

"He's out of Intensive Care. I spent a few minutes with him today, but he's still very sedated."

"Who's handling the woods for you?"

Christy cleared her throat. "For the time being Clem Molinski. You know Clem, don't you?"

"Yeah, I know him. I'm surprised you got him to agree to take on the responsibility, though."

"It's only temporary. Stubb Brannigan is . . . out of town and unaware of the situation. I expect him back anytime, and everyone thinks Stubb can take Joe's place."

"Stubb, huh? Well, maybe. He's a little careless with liquor, you know."

"Only on his own time, Rusty. Listen, you don't happen to know of a good logging superintendent out of work, do you?"

Rusty chuckled in her ear. "Good supers aren't out of work, Christy. I'll keep my eyes peeled, though, and if I hear of anyone, I'll let you know."

"Thanks. I'd appreciate it. I've called the State Employment Service but they haven't been all that encouraging either."

"Sorry to hear that. Getting back to why I called, I hope you realize I'm not trying to add to your problems right now. But we can't get by on only four loads a day."

"I know that." Deep down Christy was just a little bit elated that *any* logs had made it to the mill. Tomorrow would be better, she felt. It might take a while to get the ostensibly leaderless crew up to normal speed, but the men were trying, which raised her hopes immensely.

"Well, keep me informed," Rusty said, which was his standard sign-off. Actually, "keeping Rusty informed" was out of her hands; he saw to it that he was very well informed.

Putting the phone down, Christy raked a wisp of hair out of her eyes and sat back in her chair. The computer's cursor was blinking at her, pointing out where she had left off. She was entering checks into the accounting system and was almost finished with the task.

Throughout the job, throughout the entire day, for that matter, she had gritted her teeth over Stubb's continuing absence. Where *was* the man? If he suddenly walked through the door, she wouldn't know whether to hug him or throw something at him. How dare he ask her to wire money, then not use it to come home? Joe, himself, would be furious about such conduct.

This was Tuesday. Surely Stubb would show up before Saturday.

And if he didn't?

Away from Vince Bonnell's overpowering personality, it was all too possible to dread Saturday's planned trip to the woods. Hours together in Bonnell's truck? Or hers? The vehicle didn't matter; it was the proximity that kept gnawing at Christy. And then, once they were out there, they would be miles from anyone else. If he'd kissed her in town in broad daylight where any number of people could have seen the incident, what would he try when they were way off by themselves?

And what if she cooperated? What if she got all giddy and silly the way she had last night? Well, she hadn't really gotten giddy, but she had felt Vince's charisma deep inside of herself.

She didn't want to fall for any man right now—not with her present responsibilities—least of all one she didn't trust as far as she could throw him. After years of living alone and not at all unhappy or discontent about it, why was her darn libido suddenly coming to life? And why was it responding to Vince Bonnell, of all people?

Regardless of what she knew to be best for herself, and certainly Joe, apparently her chemistry reacted to Bonnell's. It was disgusting to be so physically uncontrolled.

Forcing her attention back to her work, Christy placed her right hand on the computer's ten-key pad and began entering numbers.

She was engrossed when the door opened and someone came in. Looking up, Christy was glad to see Clem. She stood up. "Thank you for stopping by, Clem. Would you like a cup of coffee?"

"No, I'm just here for a minute. We got four loads out today. Thought you'd wanna know."

The old man's clothing was dirty, and obviously he was just now coming off the mountain. "I know. Rusty Parnell called. But I appreciate your coming by to fill me in."

"The men are worried about Stubb. Have you heard anything from him?"

Christy's heart sank, and she sat down again slowly. She didn't want to add fuel to the fire of that dumb feud, but she couldn't keep Clem and the other men in the dark about Stubb's whereabouts, either. Of course they were worried about their co-worker and friend. If *she* hadn't heard from Stubb by now, she would certainly have notified the sheriff that he was missing.

"He's in Missoula, Montana," she said quietly.

"Missoula! What in heck's he doing in Missoula?"

Christy cleared her throat. "It's a rather involved story. Stubb should be back anytime."

Clem's pale blue eyes narrowed. "Did you talk to him?"

"He called. I...wired him money to get home on." Clem, she could see, was perplexed and curious, which was understandable. It didn't matter that she really hadn't had a choice in giving him Stubb's location; the information was going to cause trouble.

"Then he must've told you why he just up and went off without a word to anyone," Clem said with a stubborn glint in his eyes that Christy was beginning to find familiar.

She sighed and wished she could just crawl off somewhere and hide until Joe was better and everything was back in his capable hands. "He told me," she admitted, facing the futility of lying about this. When Stubb got back, he certainly wasn't going to keep the story quiet, and besides, the lies she had to tell were bad enough.

Crustily Clem exclaimed, "Well, are you gonna keep it to yourself, or what?"

As emotionlessly as possible, Christy told the tale, omitting every reference to Bonnell's men having been involved. She didn't fool Clem one little bit.

"Well, we all know who put him in that boxcar, don't we?" he said slyly.

Christy shook her head hopelessly. If she gave in to the anger swarming in her midsection, she would forever alienate this cantankerous old codger. Where was her normal patience? After only a few days in charge of the Morrison

Logging Company, she felt like firing every last one of the crew and giving them a piece of her mind along with their final paycheck, too!

Clem turned and walked to the door. "See ya tomorrow," he flung over his shoulder as he exited.

"You irritating, nasty old man," she muttered under her breath as the door slammed behind him. If he didn't go directly to the Way Inn and start some kind of ruckus about Stubb's trip to Missoula, she would be eternally astonished. All she could do was wait for the reverberations of revenge and hope that whatever the Morrison crew came up with to avenge Stubb, it wouldn't disrupt their work.

Joe was semialert when Christy walked into his room at six and even managed a weak smile. Laura was sitting in a chair beside her husband's bed. "Hi, honey," she said to her daughter.

"Hi, Mom." Christy went to the bed. "Hello, Joe. Feeling any better?"

"I'm not feeling much of anything," he mumbled thickly.

Christy smiled. "Well, I guess that's good right now."

Joe's eyelids fluttered down, then up again. "What's going on at the job?"

Maintaining her smile, Christy lied through her teeth. "Everything's fine. I've talked to Rusty Parnell several times and he's satisfied with deliveries. He asks about you every time we talk."

"If Rusty's satisfied—" Joe took a slow breath "—then everything must be all right."

Laura's wide, grateful smile gave Christy a guilty pang. They were counting on her so much, both Joe and her mother, and if she let them down, she would never get over it. With all that was going on, though, probably only a miracle would see her through.

After a minute Joe was sleeping soundly, snoring lightly. Laura stood up. "He sleeps most of the time, poor dear."

"Ready for dinner, Mom?"

Laura rubbed the back of her neck. "I'm ready to stretch my legs. Would you mind if we walked to Mabel's?"

"Not at all. I've been sitting most of the day, too."

The sky had been gray all day, but at least it wasn't raining. Leaving the hospital, they started down the block. "Mr. Bonnell stopped in again," Laura announced.

Christy nearly tripped over a twig on the sidewalk. "Did he speak to Joe?" she asked, amazed at the man's nerve.

"Joe was sleeping. I didn't know Mr. Bonnell was such a nice man. We chatted for a while, and I truly enjoyed talking to him."

"He's a charmer, all right," Christy drawled dryly.

"Does his concern bother you, Christy? It surprises me, I must admit. After he left I kept remembering little incidents and things I heard Joe saying through the years. I'm almost positive they were never friends."

"They weren't. Mom, I don't know why Bonnell is playing Mr. Nice Guy, but—"

"Oh, Christy, is that what he's doing, playing?"

Christy knew that she wasn't being entirely fair. Her attitude toward Vince Bonnell was extremely colored by personal overtones. His doing, maybe, after that kiss he'd forced on her and the smooth way he kept reminding her of it. But her reactions and responses were all her own, and not to be blamed on him or anyone else. That old saying, "you can lead a horse to water but you can't make him drink," had merit and seemed to fit her situation very well. A man could force a kiss on a woman, but he couldn't force a response from her.

The other side of his concern, sincere or not, was something she didn't want to get into with her mother. If she started explaining the worry she had about trusting Bonnell as far as his advice with the company went, Laura might catch on that her daughter's constant reassurances about the business were mostly lies.

"No, that was only a snippy remark. Please forget I said it."

"Well, it certainly would be better for all concerned if Mr. Bonnell and Joe were friends, don't you agree? They're in the same business, and it's always comforting to talk to someone who understands your own trials and tribulations."

"Very true, Mom. Here's the café. Let's have a pleasant dinner."

Christy was in her nightgown and robe when the doorbell rang that night around nine. Muffin went bonkers and yapped his way from the living room to the foyer, slipping and sliding as he rounded the corner at full speed.

Somehow she just knew who was going to be standing on her front stoop. Sure enough, when she peeked out the window, she saw Vince Bonnell. "Hush, Muffin," she said sharply, and unlocked and opened the door.

"I saw your lights."

"You do keep an eye on people's lights, don't you?"

"May I come in?"

"What for?" Christy had only opened the door a few inches, guarding her nightwear behind it.

"I didn't get a chance to call today, and I wanted to check on how things are going for you."

Apparently he was going to "check" on her every day. Christy didn't know whether to laugh or cry at so much unsolicited attention. "I have a telephone," she pointed out.

"Sure, but I was driving by—"

"Just how does such a busy man find so much time to drive around and look for lights?"

Vince laughed. "You're sure a suspicious little thing. Heard anything from Stubb?"

Stubb's name brought back her conversation with Clem. "He's not back yet that I know of, but Clem questioned me today and I had to tell him about Stubb's little trip."

"Oh-oh. Guess my crew can start watching for some kind of retribution from Morrison employees."

"That whole thing makes me sick!"

"Why should it? They're just having fun."

"Your idea of fun is light-years away from mine."

"What *is* your idea of fun?" he asked with a sassy grin. Muffin had been trying, and finally succeeded in maneuvering around Christy's legs. Vince spotted the little terrier. "Hello, what's this? I thought I heard a dog." He stooped and held out his hand. "Take a sniff, boy. Let's be pals."

Muffin, the little traitor, licked Vince's hand. Peevishly Christy said, "Bite him, Muffin."

Vince roared with laughter. "If Muffin's your idea of an attack dog..."

The man was impossible. He laughed too easily, as though he truly enjoyed every dumb thing she said. Actually, she would have given Muffin double rations of dog biscuits for a week if he would have taken just a tiny nip out of Bonnell.

"You sure do get a kick out of me, don't you? I've never been around anyone who thought everything I said was funny."

Standing up, Vince leaned against the door frame. "Guess what? I've never been around anyone who made me feel so good. *That's* why I laugh with you."

"*I* make you feel good?" Christy said doubtfully, and then a shiver ran up her spine. His expression had changed completely, taking on that sensual look she'd seen several times by now.

"I could make you feel good, too," he said softly. "Invite me in, Christy."

Her temperature soared, just as surely as if a sudden fever had struck her system. All sorts of erotic images flashed through her mind one after the other—hot, greedy, openmouthed kisses, naked, writhing, intertwined bodies.

She had lived alone much too long.

Drawing the lapels of her robe together with one nervous hand, Christy kept a rather shaky grip on the door with the other. "That's a crude suggestion," she croaked hoarsely. "Please leave."

She attempted to close the door, but then Muffin suddenly darted through the opening. And Vince had left the gate open! "Now see what you've done!" she cried as the little terrier shot down the walk and into the street.

Forgetting her bathrobe and bare feet, Christy threw the door open and ran past Vince. "Muffin! Come back here, Muffin!"

Vince jogged behind her. He saw the joyful leaps Muffin was making. "He's only playing with you."

"Which I don't need right now! Why did you leave the darn gate open? Muffin! Come here!" Christy trailed after Muffin, coaxing him to come to her. The asphalt was cold and damp on her bare feet. "Oh, no, he's going to the park," she groaned.

Bounding from the street, Muffin gained the grass of the small park, where Christy often took him for a walk. He stopped to sniff every bush, but stayed well ahead of his pursuers.

"You must keep him closed up too much," Vince commented.

"I most certainly do not! He has a doggie door and full run of the yard. Muffin! We're not playing tonight. Come back here!"

Vince chuckled at the terrier's antics. The little pooch was having a great time, running and barking, then stopping at one bush after another. His timing was perfect. He was teasing Christy and inviting her to play, and it was all pretty funny.

But Vince's chuckles and obvious amusement earned him only dirty looks from Christy. The grass was wet and cold on her feet, and she saw nothing funny about running after Muffin in her bathrobe.

Vince stopped her with a hand on her arm. "This isn't working. Muffin thinks you're playing and you're not going to catch him this way. I'll go around the park and come at him from the other direction. We'll get him in between us."

"Fine," she agreed tersely, wondering who she was more upset with—Bonnell or Muffin.

"Walk slowly," Vince instructed as he moved away. "Lull him into thinking you don't care if you catch him or not."

"I suppose you're an expert on dog behavior, too," she mumbled under her breath. But Vince's suggestion, irritating or not, made sense, and she advanced at a slower pace. Almost immediately, Christy saw, Muffin sensed the game had changed. The little dog looked at her quizzically, turning his head to one side and then the other.

Vince made a wide sweep of the park's perimeter and nonchalantly approached Muffin from behind while Christy got closer from her direction. Then Muffin caught on and looked back at Vince. His little ears perked up and he barked excitedly. Christy was barely two feet away, and she made a dive at Muffin, who darted away at the last second. Off balance, Christy went sprawling and skidded along the wet grass on her belly.

She sat up and wailed right out loud. Her robe was soaked, her feet were freezing, Muffin was looking at her from twenty feet away and Vince was whooping with laughter.

Again that urge to either laugh or cry hit her, and for some crazy reason her system chose laughter. It was maybe the most idiotic moment of her entire life, but once she emitted the first hoot of laughter, *everything* seemed funny, Muffin, Vince and especially herself.

Tears rolled down her face, but the only thing that didn't seem hilarious about the past four days was Joe's accident, and her and Vince Bonnell's laughter mingled and destroyed the park's quiet. The final straw was Muffin docilely walking up and licking her chin. Throwing her arms around the mischievous little terrier, Christy hugged him and laughed again.

Vince walked up and held out a hand. "Come on. You're wet clear through. Let's get you home."

Christy willingly allowed him to help pull her to her feet, but when he swept her up off the ground and into his arms, she protested. "I can walk!"

"Of course you can." Vince headed for the street. "You're capable of doing anything you want to do." He grinned. "Aren't you?"

She put her arms around his neck and wove her fingers together, merely a means of steadying her precarious position, she told herself. "You're making fun of me."

"You should laugh more often. You've got a great laugh."

"Nothing has struck me very funny lately. I think I got a little hysterical just now. Where's Muffin?" she asked, looking around. "Oh, there he is." The little terrier was following as meekly as a lamb. "You naughty boy," Christy scolded.

"Am I a naughty boy, too?"

Christy looked at Vince. Their faces were an inch apart. He was carrying her as effortlessly as she carried Muffin on occasion, and she felt Bonnell's strength and size in every cell of her body. "I think you like that idea," she accused.

A grin tugged at his lips. "Sometimes naughty is nice." His gaze found hers, and all signs of humor disappeared from his expression. "*You're* nice. Womanly, firm, warm."

Christy swallowed. Vince was getting to her, as he always did. "And wet," she reminded in a near whisper.

"You'll probably never get the grass stains out of this robe."

She made a small throat-clearing sound. "Probably not."

He made her feel very adult and something else, something she couldn't quite grasp. Glamorous? She discarded the word. Sophisticated? That wasn't right, either. The sensation was very female, very mature, but new to her, apparently a completely unique response to this particular man.

He wanted her, or seemed to. Christy was almost positive that she could feel his desire. And somehow she knew there would be nothing childlike or uncertain in Vince Bonnell's lovemaking. Her body tingled at the images flooding her mind, him naked and aroused, herself naked and inviting.

She drew a softly shuddering breath, and Vince brought her closer to his chest, snuggling her, cradling her. "You frighten me," she whispered, wishing to God that was all there was to this. Ordinary fright she could deal with. What Vince made her feel—and worry about—was clouded with layers of suspicion.

"I know." Vince walked through her gate with Muffin on his heels. "Latch it," he murmured, tipping Christy so that she could reach the latch.

Having Vince "know" her feelings was as intimate as his touch and just as disturbing. "You can put me down now," she told him.

"In the house." The door had been left wide open, and Vince walked through it, made sure Muffin had come in, too, then closed the door with the press of one shoulder. The lighted foyer revealed Christy's wet and grass-stained robe, but Vince gave it only a cursory glance, then stared into her eyes.

"I . . . do not want an affair," she said, speaking as normally as she could manage. Which wasn't all that great sounding when she heard herself. Her heart was hammering and what could she do about it? What could she do about any of her reactions to this man?

"Don't label it. Don't question it. Don't be afraid."

She tried to laugh and failed miserably. "Easy to say."

He brought his face closer to hers and saw the slight parting of her lips and then the tip of her tongue. There was something bleak in her eyes, a resignation that whatever was happening was beyond her control. It didn't hinder Vince's ardor, nor give him any guilt, although he understood her dislike of the word *affair.*

But that was where they were heading. He couldn't think beyond that right now. At this stage of a relationship no one could predict its outcome. He only knew that he wanted this small sexy woman, and she wanted him, too, despite having reservations. It was enough for now.

His mouth opened on hers, and at her breathy response, he slipped his tongue between her lips. Her arms tightened around his neck, and the kiss deepened into roughness, into overwhelming heat and groping desire. He adjusted their positions, letting her legs slide down his body, but holding her up and to himself so that her feet were dangling off the floor.

The curves of her body, so ill-defined in that robe, were suddenly his to know, and her small breasts burned his chest. Kissing her again and again, licking her lips, sucking on her tongue, knowing that she was gasping and panting and kissing him back, he went into the opening of her robe, found the hem of her short nightgown and burrowed beneath it.

And then he made contact with his goal—the soft hair at the base of her belly, the female moisture between her thighs.

"No, wait," she gasped.

"Baby...sweetheart..." His voice was thick and hoarse. He was in flames, almost crazed with need.

She hadn't been prepared for such uninhibited wildness. A kiss maybe, but not this. "Vince...no!"

Breathing hard, he raised his head and let her ease downward. Her feet touched the floor, and she reeled and clutched at his shirt for support. His eyes were glazed and partially hooded. "Christy..."

She tried to back up, but his hands were on her shoulders. "I won't behave this way."

Something snapped in Vince. Christy had made their "behavior" sound almost disgusting, as though they had no right to passion. "No? How do you like it—with lukewarm kisses and the lights out? This is the real thing, honey, the kind of emotion that goes on between grown-ups. Maybe you're not up to it."

"Maybe I'm not," she whispered shakily. Taking her hands away from his chest, she retied the loosened sash of her robe. "I think you'd better leave."

Vince was watching her closely, trying to figure her out. "Maybe I went too fast. I'm not normally so eager, Christy. You affect the hell out of me. That's my only defense."

Oddly she felt an apology welling, too. "I'm not used to—"

"My kind of man?"

She flicked one very confused glance to his eyes. "I don't know what kind of man you are, so how could I answer that?"

He reached out and caught the back of her head in his big hand. "Look at me." When she did, a trifle defiantly, he took a deep, labored breath. He would feel on edge for a long time because of what had just taken place. So quickly, within the space of mere heartbeats, he had gone from normal desire to desperation. As he'd told her, they were dealing with very grown-up emotions, but pressing that point would only make her more uncomfortable than she already was.

"You do know me," he said distinctly. "There's no secret man hiding beneath the surface. What you see, and what you've learned about me in the past few days, is what I am. What just happened between us might not have been exactly what you expected, but it's nothing to be ashamed of, and I'm not. It did teach me one thing—to take it a little slower with you. But I'm not going to stand here and pretend to want you any less." His eyes narrowed. "And it is going to happen, Christy. One of these days you won't say no."

He smiled then, relaxing some, reminding her of the laughter they had shared in the park. "I'll say good-night now." Pulling her forward, he planted a kiss on her forehead, held her head to his chest for a moment, then released her. "I'll either call or drop by the office tomorrow."

Christy locked the door behind him. Her legs felt all rubbery and weak, although her pulse seemed inordinately strong. Stumbling through the house, with Muffin trailing behind, she turned off the lights and ended up in her bedroom. After shedding her damp robe and nightgown, she pulled a fresh gown out of the dresser drawer and dropped it over her head.

Snapping off the light, she crawled into bed. Her pulse was still stronger than it should be. No one had ever kissed her quite like that. Nor taken her response as permission to do whatever he pleased with her body.

Alone, she was able to think about Bonnell's big hand under her nightgown. What if she hadn't stopped him? What if she had opened her legs and let him explore? A shiver prickled her skin, which was in exact opposition to the searing flame in her loins.

She began weeping quietly. *One of these days you won't say no.* Vince was right. One of these days she *wouldn't* say no.

And then where would she be?

Six

By Friday evening Christy knew she was in deep trouble. Clem had belligerently threatened to quit his job if she didn't find someone else to foreman the operation, and there was no one else. Log deliveries were sporadic and sparse. Rusty was on the phone twice a day complaining, and not only him. The truck drivers, who were making very little money, were griping, too.

Actually, the whole crew seemed to be falling apart, and if that wasn't enough to make Christy's hair stand on end, she had yelled at Clem. But when he announced—rather blasély, Christy had thought—that he was going to the hospital to talk to Joe about everything, *including* Stubb's absence... well, she just lost control.

She had turned on the old logger with eyes blazing. "Go and see Joe. I know he would appreciate seeing you and anyone else who might drop by. But if you breathe one word about Stubb being gone and just how bad things are in the woods, I'll make you sorry you were ever born!"

Clem had backed up three full steps. "Well, heck, you don't have to get so riled."

"I'm *very* riled. And please pass the message on to the other men. No one better bring Joe any sad stories or tales of woe! I mean it, Clem. I've been telling Joe everything is going just fine, and I don't want you or anyone else making me out a liar. Joe has all he can do to get well. He doesn't need to lie there in that bed and worry about something he can't do a thing about!"

Clem had gone off muttering to himself, and Christy could only hope the stubborn old coot wouldn't go directly to Joe and sing his sad song.

By Friday, though, she realized Joe hadn't heard any disturbing information about his business. He was a little more alert each time Christy visited him, but he seemed unusually disinterested in precise questions. He trusted her to keep everything rolling, she decided, which made her more determined than ever to do so.

Which also meant, she finally accepted as final, a trip to the mountain with Vince Bonnell. Maybe he could fill her in on how to organize the crew. Stubb, blast his careless soul, still hadn't shown up, and Christy swore that when he finally wandered in, he was going to get an earful.

She was getting tougher, which totally amazed her. She'd always assumed she had many of her mother's gentle tendencies, but circumstances, she was discovering, were bringing out a resistant nature she hadn't even suspected she possessed. Apparently her hide was a lot thicker than she'd thought. Lambasting Clem was proof of that.

And then there was Vince keeping her awake nights. Thankfully he hadn't dropped in again. She could deal with his forceful personality on the phone a lot easier than she could in person, and she was darn worried about spending Saturday with him.

But she honestly didn't know what else to do. The thing was, as important as Morrison Logging Company—and Vince's company, too, for that matter—was to the local economy, neither company could compete for top-notch employees with the major logging firms in the state. As Rusty had pointed out so succinctly, good supers weren't out of work. Vince was lucky to have the excellent foreman he had. Men of that caliber weren't wandering Oregon's back roads looking for a job.

Aside from all of those purely commonsense facts roaming her brain, however, Christy felt painfully vulnerable. Was she destined to be the sacrifice upon Bonnell's altar of greed? Was he merely using her to sabotage Joe's job? How could she go out to the woods with him and trust what he told her? On the other hand, who knew the complete picture better than a successful logging company owner? And what if, by the slimmest chance, Vince *wasn't* trying to deceive anyone? What if the man was truly trying to help?

There was something about the overall situation that made Christy realize she had to distance her own torn-up personal feelings from everything else going on. She had to glean information where she could from whoever offered it. If Vince was using her to keep abreast of Joe's operation, it would eventually come out. All she could do in the meantime was to stay alert, and away from Bonnell's kisses!

Vince called the office Friday afternoon. "How about having supper together tonight?"

Just the sound of his deep voice on the phone did peculiar things to Christy, but she felt like a sneak as it was. Joe and Vince weren't friends, and there was no ignoring the fact that Vince hadn't gone back to the hospital since Joe had become more alert. That was evidence enough for Christy that Vince knew darn well Joe wouldn't welcome his intrusion into Morrison affairs.

And announcing her disloyalty to the whole town by publicly sharing a meal with Vince Bonnell was going too far. "You know I can't do that," she said into the phone.

"I thought that feud made you sick."

"It does. But like it or not, you and I are on opposite sides of it."

"Are you saying you'll never go out with me?"

"Vince, please don't push."

"You still don't trust me, do you?"

Lord, if only she could. But she dare not forget the nebulous hold she had on Joe's contract at the present. How long would Rusty accept short deliveries before he canceled Joe's contract and reissued it to Bonnell Logging Company? Christy had gotten out that contract and read it through, and it looked to her as if Rennard Lumber Company had a powerful upper hand. There was little in the clauses to protect Joe, and paragraph after paragraph protected Rennard.

Outside of personal distress she didn't even want to think about, it all boiled down to loyalty, and every drop of hers was directed to Joe. Which really did make her feel like a sneak. Looking to Vince for advice while swearing loyalty to Joe was like having two opposing personalities.

"I trust you to give me good advice tomorrow," she said, crossing her fingers and holding her breath with the lie.

Vince completely eluded the subject. "How about me picking up a couple of steaks and a bottle of wine and coming to your house for supper? Do you have a barbecue grill?"

"Yes, I have a barbecue grill," Christy replied uneasily. "But I've been having dinner with Mom every night."

"She won't miss you for one night, and I've been missing you since Tuesday."

"No, I really can't tonight."

"Then tomorrow night. Count on it, Christy. When we get back to town tomorrow, we'll have sup...dinner together. At my place."

"Your place?"

"Do you know where I live?"

She knew, but she didn't want to admit she did. "Somewhere out of town, I think."

"Well, that doesn't matter. I'll be doing the driving. What time do you want me to pick you up in the morning?"

"It's probably best if I meet you somewhere."

"So your neighbors won't catch on? What did you tell them about running around in your bathrobe with me on Tuesday night?"

"No one mentioned it."

He chuckled in her ear. "Thinking you're fooling anyone in this town is pretty naive, Christy. I might as well drive right up to your front door. Someone's bound to see us together tomorrow."

"And that doesn't bother you?"

"Not in the least. I'd be proud to be seen with you anywhere, at anytime, by anyone, honey."

Vince Bonnell tangled her emotions in a way no one ever had. That divided personality she'd been thinking about was beginning to pinch. How could she like a man she couldn't trust? How could she want him?

Vince made her blood race, he raised her temperature, he made her tingle and ache and imagine the craziest scenarios. And she had thought she'd been content to live alone and experience life through novels and television.

She'd been living a secondhand existence, with surreptitious thrills and a buried consciousness, a poor substitute for what Vince made her feel.

All right, so she was ready to admit the man had gotten under her skin. In a purely sexual context, of course. But what, under the present circumstances, could she do about it?

"That's very flattering," Christy replied. "But I would like to meet you somewhere just the same. How about the first turnoff from the highway?" She heard a long sigh of resignation.

"All right, fine. What time?"

"Eight?"

"Eight, it is. See you then."

The morning's eerily bright and patchy fog promised sunshine, which elated Christy. Demanding calmness from her central nervous system, vowing to look at the day ahead with an intelligent, mature point of view, she dressed in jeans and two different shirts, a layered effect in case it got warm enough later on to shed one.

Brushing her hair, Christy decided she didn't want it flopping around all day. Gathering it into a thick handful at the back of her head, she fashioned a fat braid, securing the end of it with a rubber band. She went very easy on the makeup, using only light touches of blusher and lip gloss.

With her purse containing a notebook and pen, Christy bade Muffin goodbye and left the house. The drive to the designated meeting spot would take about twenty minutes, and she turned on the radio, hoping to get caught up in music rather than another bout of apprehension over Vince Bonnell.

He was becoming a constant companion, underlying every other thought or activity, a dismaying, unnerving state to find herself seemingly locked into. On one hand she had every right to a personal relationship with a man, and not only that, it was probably time she did. But why Bonnell? Why was he the first man to appeal to her in so many years?

The music helped but couldn't completely squelch the questions, and Christy drove with a frown of concentration.

When she arrived at the turnoff, Vince's truck was already there. Christy pulled off the road and parked beneath the spreading branches of an enormous oak tree. Vince ambled over, wearing a smile that sent ripples of awareness throughout Christy's ambivalent system.

"Morning," he greeted. "We're going to have some sunshine today."

Christy climbed down from the cab of Joe's pickup. "It appears that way."

"You should have brought Muffin along. He'd have a great time running through the woods."

"Oh, Lord, no. He'd be full of burrs and ticks tonight. Do you want to drive, or shall I?" Just seeing the man, being with him, was physically energizing. Rationale seemed totally ineffective with Bonnell. With his size and ruggedness enhanced by work clothes—jeans, boots, a black-and-white plaid flannel shirt—he could be an advertisement for the ultimate outdoors male.

"What've you done to your hair?" Vince took her chin and turned her head. "Oh, it's in a braid. For a second there I thought you'd chopped it off."

The momentary note of panic in his voice gave Christy a start. Would it really matter to him if she cut her hair?

She stepped back, breaking contact. "You can drive. If you don't mind, that is."

"Whichever you prefer."

All the while Vince's gray eyes kept moving over her. Not with lewdness nor unnecessary delays at the more female portions of her anatomy. But along with a twinkle—maybe only because sunshine seemed imminent—Bonnell's eyes radiated excitement.

And affection. And masculine acknowledgment and appreciation. There was a gladness about him, a sparkle that had nothing to do with sunlit fog.

Should she believe it? Ignore it? Should she pretend not to understand? Her own pulse was beating in a strange, lilting manner, which was impossible to ignore. Pretense, however, was *entirely* possible.

Christy abruptly turned back to her pickup, explaining as she walked away, "I'll get my purse." And then a whole new aspect of this exercise struck her. Maybe Clem could do the same thing Vince was planning, give her pointers on how to run the operation. Christy realized instantly that the conjecture was belated and should have been considered before this.

Sighing, she retrieved her purse from the seat of the pickup. She hadn't thought of asking Clem's advice, probably because the old man was so doggone cantankerous and opposed to added responsibility. Then, too, Vince had been there offering help.

Whatever, she was out here with Vince, and calling the day off now would not only be awkward, but she really had no instinct with Clem. He might balk at doing anything other than his regular job as boom operator, even something as undemanding as this, giving her a lesson in logging procedures.

They got into Vince's truck and started up the mountain. "Still no word from Stubb?" Vince inquired casually.

"Nothing." Vince began to chuckle, and Christy gave him a curious look. "Something funny about that?"

"I was thinking about what happened to Sonny Brogan Thursday night."

"He works for you, doesn't he?" Christy saw Vince's nod, then felt a premonition. "Wait a minute. Did Joe's crew do something to Sonny because of what your men did to Stubb?"

Vince took his eyes off the road and gave her a grin. "Apparently you didn't hear about it."

"Apparently not."

"Lighten up, Christy. It's nothing to get uptight about. Actually, it's almost as funny as Stubb ending up in a boxcar in Missoula."

Christy's lips had tensed to a thin line. "I can't believe grown men behave so childishly. What happened?"

There was laughter in Vince's voice. "The ladies of the Rock Falls Community Church hold a meeting every Thursday evening in the basement of the church. At their last meeting they had an uninvited guest."

"Sonny?"

"It went like this. Sonny was all beered up and fell asleep in his chair. A couple of Morrison men saw their chance and took Sonny over to the church. I don't know how they talked him out of his pants, but they shoved him through the door of the meeting room in his boxer shorts."

"Oh, honestly," Christy groaned.

"That's not the funny part. The ladies threw him back out the door—bodily—but on the way out he got whacked with whatever the ladies could get their hands on. I understand that most of the weapons were purses." Vince was grinning from ear to ear. "By the way, his boxers were red with black polka dots."

The scene was vivid in Christy's mind, and she didn't want to laugh about something so moronic. But Sonny Brogan had a bald head and a large, rotund belly, and envisioning him in polka-dotted red shorts and being driven from the church by purse-wielding women was pure slapstick comedy.

Christy suddenly found herself struggling to maintain a straight face. Laughing about such idiotic behavior was the same as condoning it, which she certainly didn't do. Secondly, and maybe more crucial to her own peace of mind, laughing with Vince Bonnell could become habit forming.

Regardless, her smile turned into a laugh, sensible or not. Fueling the giggle threatening her composure was Vince's unrestrained laughter. He did love a joke, apparently, and darn if it wasn't catching!

He began naming the ladies involved, and Christy almost choked. "Not Mrs. Carew!" she exclaimed, seeing the buxom, very straitlaced lady in the middle of the melee as hilarious.

"And the parson's wife."

"Oh, no!"

"Sonny was mighty red-faced at work yesterday."

Calming down, Christy sighed. "It's all so silly. But," she added with an eye on Vince, "at least Sonny was still available for work after the gag. Who knows where Stubb is?"

Vince returned her look, but only briefly as the mountain road needed almost constant attention. Christy was extremely judgmental on the matter of Stubb, and Vince wasn't all that positive now that his men *had* been involved. "None of my men admit to putting Stubb in that boxcar."

"Well, they did it!"

"Presumably. Even I thought so when you first told me about it. But now I'm not so sure. With every other prank, Christy, the instigators boasted. Take that incident Thursday evening, for example. Everyone knows who shoved Sonny into that meeting room. Stubb's misadventure now, no one knows any more about it than that he ended up—"

"Vince, he didn't just wander into that boxcar on his own!" Bonnell's intimations of innocence were preposterous. Of course his men were responsible.

"I certainly don't want to get into a hassle with you about it," Vince declared. "But try to keep an open mind on the subject, will you? The men see these stunts as funny and love to take credit for one. It seems a little odd to me that no one has bragged about it being his idea."

"Those men have a warped sense of humor!"

"Just because it's different than yours?"

Christy stiffened. "I know you get a big bang out of the two crews picking on each other, but I find their behavior adolescent and ridiculous!"

With an amused grin Vince shook his head. "Come on now, didn't you just laugh about Sonny's little escapade?"

"One of these days a joke will backfire and someone will get hurt. Would it be so funny then?"

Vince sobered. "Of course not. But these men work hard, and if they let off a little steam playing jokes on one another, where's the harm?"

Christy turned in the seat to look at Vince. "You want to discuss 'harm'? What about my being without a foreman because of Stubb's unplanned trip to Montana? You and I wouldn't be on our way to Joe's logging site right now without one of those stupid jokes."

A lazy grin appeared on Vince's face. "Christy, if you think I'm sitting here regretting this trip, forget that notion. Joe's accident was unfortunate—calamitous for him, tragic for your mother. But one good thing came out of it— you and me getting to know each other."

Why, in God's name, was she blushing? How did this man have the power to turn her anger—*justified* anger—into something personal? He was clever at manipulating the conversation, and what else was he clever at?

Christy's spine softened. He would be good in bed, very expert, very ardent. Sometimes—rarely, in her case—a woman knew things about a man. Instinct, probably. Intuition. Whatever, this bear of a man, this *bull* of a man, seemed to want her, and his cleverness was making her want him, too.

He was driving, looking at the road, and his expression, in profile, seemed incredibly sensual. Unless she was imagining things. Unless she was seeing her own feelings.

Christy's scrutiny was impossible to miss, which broadened Vince's smile. He was beginning to understand her. She didn't want to like him and she did. She didn't want to trust him, but her reasons for caution were losing distinction. Then, too, the strong sexuality between them puzzled and frightened her. Maybe *frightened* wasn't the best word, but she was definitely wary of their chemistry.

Vince's thoughts became explicit. He wanted to make love to her, to undress her and love her until they were both weak. But he was so big and she was so small. He would have to be very gentle with her.

She was still staring. "Like what you're seeing?" he asked softly, daring her to be honest.

Her tongue traced her dry lips. "You're a good-looking man," she conceded.

"Was that what you were studying so intently—the way I look? I don't think so, Christy. You're having trouble with feelings, the ones you're picking up from me as well as your own."

They had reached the final turn, the last stretch of road before the logging site. Vince stopped the truck and put the gearshift into park. Swiveling, he stretched an arm along the top of the seat back and faced her.

Christy swallowed with an instant attack of nerves. "We're almost there. Why did you stop?" He moved across the seat, coming closer. "Vince, I didn't come out here to—"

His hand lifted to cup her chin. "Do you know how pretty you are?" She frowned, because she didn't believe she was pretty. Interesting, maybe. Striking, with the right clothes and makeup. But not pretty.

His gaze roamed her features. "Can you honestly say you're sorry that circumstances brought us together? I can't. I'm sorry Joe got hurt, but there's a logical part of my brain that knows without his accident you and I might have lived the rest of our lives without ever speaking to each other."

He lowered his face. "And that would have been a hell of a waste, honey. Let me kiss you."

Let him? Christy stared into his dark gray eyes. Did he mean that if she said no, he *wouldn't* kiss her? It would be that simple?

Nothing was ever simple, though, especially male-female relationships. Her past, her way of life and her own feelings were in the path of common sense. She was hungry for a man's touch, although she hadn't realized it. Nor would just any man do.

But this one would. This man made her feel alive in a way she had almost forgotten existed. He was waiting for a sign, his mouth an inch from hers. She could feel his breath and smell his scent, and her own blood pressure was becoming a roar in her ears.

Her lips parted, an invitation that made Vince's heart pound. He looked down at her for another moment, then slowly fit his mouth to hers. The breath seemed to rush out of Christy in one big sigh as a most delicious weakness spread throughout her limbs and body. There was something relieving about ignoring the warnings in the back of her mind. Since Bonnell had first shown up at the hospital, those warnings had been persistent and irritating, and it felt good to push them aside and follow her own urges.

She opened her lips wider for Vince's tongue, which he used to stroke the soft interior of her mouth. Actions became involuntary then, movements to attain closeness. Her arms went up around his neck, while his gathered her into a tight embrace. Her breasts were flattened by the pressure of his chest, and the air was turbulent with gasping breaths and throaty sounds of pleasure.

The pickup's engine was still running, a low, humming vibration. Turning himself and Christy, Vince reached out and switched off the ignition, then brought Christy onto his lap, placing her in the cradle of his arms and body. He licked her lips before kissing them again, and was so elated that she was kissing him back that he began to wonder about that vow to be gentle.

How did a man stay controlled when he was holding the sweetest, sexiest little woman he'd ever known? When her lips were warm and soft and pliant beneath his, and her firm little breasts were burning holes into his chest? He could feel her nipples, twin bumps of female arousal, and knew his own arousal, much larger and extremely obvious, had to be heating her backside.

Christy was dazed and knew it. She was behaving foolishly and knew that, too. Sitting on a man's lap and glorying in the sensation of hot, wet kisses, harsh breathing and the marvel of his anatomy was like waving a red flag at a bull.

Lord, that was exactly what she was doing! She spoke, hoarsely, breathlessly, her lips moving on his. "We've got to stop."

His hand slipped under her shirts, both of them, encountered the bare skin of her waist and began to explore. "Why?" he whispered. Her long-lashed, gray-green eyes were glazed, beautifully female, slightly feverish-looking. "Why do we have to stop?" he questioned again when she didn't answer.

"Because..." Christy turned her head enough to separate their mouths. "Please..." Her heart was hammering, and the big hand moving under her shirts was only increasing its forceful beat.

"We're both free and past the age of consent," Vince reminded.

"There are other factors just as important," she whispered.

He found a breast and eased the soft elastic band of her brassiere up over it. Then, staring into her eyes, he caressed the hard little bud of her nipple. "Let's go to my place," he whispered urgently. "We can come back here this afternoon. I'm burning up."

He was. She could feel the searing heat of his manhood right through two pairs of jeans, his and hers. And the raw emotion on his face, and the thrills spiking through her body because of his fingers on her breast were very persuasive.

Christy closed her eyes, but blocking out sight didn't deter her feelings. She wanted what he did—to be naked and in bed together. To touch and taste and just let go of inhibitions and restraint. Related thoughts flicked through her mind. He would be magnificent without clothes. He would take up most of the bed. He would be heavy...and big...and...

But if they left now, they wouldn't come back. Not today. She wasn't only being foolish; she was risking Joe's business. And she dare not risk the business, not for any reason, but there was something particularly unpalatable about forgetting duty and responsibility to make love with Joe's competitor.

Drawing a deep, ragged breath, Christy sat up and removed the big hand from under her shirts. Vince stopped her from slipping from his lap, giving her a long, penetrating look. "I want you more than I've ever wanted a woman."

She couldn't allow herself to believe his glib phrases, although he looked sincere. His lips were still wet from their kisses and his face was slightly flushed. Attempting to straighten her clothing, Christy gave him only a quick glance. "I'd rather not talk about it."

"Do you think these feelings are going to disappear just because we don't talk about them?"

She became defensive. "It's all so simple for you, isn't it?"

"Is it so complex for you?"

"You're not a bit naive, so don't pretend not to know where I'm coming from."

Vince put his head back with a groan. "Not that damn feud." He let her move off his lap, although he stayed in the middle of the seat, giving her very little room in which to withdraw from him.

"No, it's not that 'damn feud,'" she said evenly, priding herself on speaking without tremors when his thigh was crowding hers. "It's Joe in the hospital and helpless. It's the business he's spent his whole life building. It's you being Joe's competitor and my needing your help. It's loyalty and Stubb's absence and the whole darn mess. And it's one thing more—a question of just how deeply I want to get involved with . . . any man."

Vince's head jerked up. "That wasn't what you were going to say."

"What?"

"You said 'any man,' but you meant me."

The conversation was getting entirely too heavy, and Christy sighed with its weight. "I don't know what I meant, all right? If you still want to give me some pointers on the logging business, let's go and get it done. Otherwise, let's go back to town."

Vince tried to stare her down, but decided he'd be wiser to fail at that endeavor. "Fine. Let's get going."

Eyeing him suspiciously as he got back behind the wheel, Christy asked, "Which direction?"

He shaped a small, wry grin. "To the woods, honey. After that, who knows?"

Seven

Vince looked everything over, walking around the clearing and silent equipment with an air of concentration. His gaze moved over the piles of logs awaiting transportation, then to Christy. "Good timber," he commented. "Let's take a walk."

"To where?"

"See those cables? They'll lead us to the present logging area."

"Oh, of course." Christy knew the equipment was moved periodically. When one area was logged out, everything had to be shifted to a fresh, uncut stand of timber. Since Joe's accident, there hadn't been enough trees removed from this particular site to warrant a move, which was a rather sad commentary on the situation.

The fog was quickly dispersing, remaining only in pockets of dense foliage. The woods were gorgeous, quiet and still, with beams of piercingly bright sunlight filtering through the trees. Following Vince, Christy watched him stop from time to time and gaze up at the tall Douglas firs. "Great timber," he remarked again, speaking reflectively, almost to himself. At one point, however, he asked Christy directly, "How many acres does Joe have in his contract?"

The question struck Christy as nosy and unnecessary to this teaching session, but she didn't want to start finding fault with Vince's methods. "Eighty in this phase."

"And how many phases?"

Christy cleared her throat, which sounded like reluctance even to herself. She saw Vince's eyes narrow. "Joe's got a long-term contract, doesn't he?"

"Yes," she admitted after another hesitation. Joe's contract wasn't neutral territory and they shouldn't be discussing it. Without strict compliance that contract wouldn't be worth the paper it was written on, which Vince knew as well as her. It was a strong point of dissension for Christy and the primary cause of the mistrust she couldn't quite get past with Vince.

He glanced around again. "My timber's not nearly this good," he said thoughtfully. "Well, let's get started."

"Yes, please," she responded quickly, glad to drop the subject of Joe's contract.

"The logging process starts here," Vince began, indicating several downed trees.

"I understand that. What's got me stymied is how to deal with the men. I know the trees are sawed down, then limbed and bucked. I know that the logs are skidded to the landing and stacked until they're loaded onto trucks. I understand the logistics of the operation, but how does one keep it all running smoothly?"

"For the most part, the crew knows what has to be done."

"Granted, but why don't they just do it?"

"In this instance it's because Joe kept such a heavy hand on the operation. No one but him ever made any decisions, and there are decisions cropping up all the time. For example, one absentee crew member can throw the entire job off balance. Stubb being gone has probably done a lot of damage to the rhythm of the overall job.''

They were moving through the woods at a leisurely pace, ducking low branches and brush. ''What you need to do is talk to the men. Find out which of them can do more than one job. That's information Joe has down pat, you can bet. You've got your sawyers, your skidders, your truck drivers, your…'' Vince ticked off each of the job titles. ''You've got to be able to move the crew around, stir the pot, so to speak, if someone doesn't show up for work.''

''You really do think I can come out here and direct Joe's men, don't you?''

Vince stopped and looked down at her. ''Yes, I do.''

Christy stared up at him, fascinated by the play of light in his gray eyes. ''What if they refuse to work for me?''

''Why would they refuse? They'll probably bust their britches to work for such a pretty boss.''

His reference to ''pretty'' gave Christy pause. He wouldn't keep on saying that if he thought otherwise, would he? There was such a sincere ring to his voice, and she was beginning to grasp just how much she wanted to believe everything he said.

''I hardly think Clem is very affected by me,'' Christy drawled dryly.

Vince grinned. ''Clem's eyesight must be failing. Mine's in great shape, by the way.'' He stepped closer. ''Christy…''

She backed up. ''No, Vince. Please, let's do what we came out here to do.''

''Maybe that's what I am doing.''

She felt something warm zing through her system. He was looking at her with desire again, with his eyes hot and full of it. ''Please don't look at me like that,'' she pleaded in a near whisper.

''How am I looking at you?''

She tried to lighten the moment with a laugh. ''Admitting you came out here to talk me into something isn't very gentlemanly.''

"Is that the kind of man you like—the gentlemanly type?"

"I try not to put people into slots, Vince." Turning, Christy started back to the landing. "What else should I know? About the job," she added hastily, thinking he might be only too happy to give her a lesson in lovemaking.

Vince grinned knowingly. "There are several crucial points—equipment maintenance for one."

"Joe has always kept a detailed record book on the equipment's maintenance."

"Good. Just follow his practices."

They had reached the edge of the clearing. Spotting a squat, wide stump, Christy sat down on it. She was worried. What was she learning that she hadn't already known? How could one person instill managerial ability in another, anyway? It was a skill that really came out of experience, or through extensive education. Even if Vince was completely sincere in trying to help, she wasn't a very confident pupil.

"Don't look so stricken," Vince teased.

She couldn't deny the charge and knew that her inner conflict had to be plastered all over her face.

"There's no reason to be scared, Christy. Get hold of Clem tomorrow and tell him you'll be on the job Monday morning. He can spread the word among the crew, and there won't be any surprised faces when you show up. Take a few minutes and talk to the men individually. Learn their strong points. I guarantee they won't be reluctant to detail their skills and job preferences. Don't be afraid to give orders, but be sure of yourself before you do."

Christy rolled her eyes. "There's the bind. If I was working with computer operators or bookkeepers, I'd be very sure of myself. Out here... ?"

"You're afraid of the men, aren't you?"

Christy frowned. "I'm sure you find that hard to understand. And maybe *intimidated* is a better word."

Vince walked a small circle, then stopped right in front of Christy. "I can only give you a pep talk, not courage. But don't you think Joe's crew understands the situation? Every single one of those men wants his job. If he didn't, he would have already quit and gone to work for someone else. Especially the truck drivers. Think about it. With few log deliveries the truckers are making very little money. They probably don't know which way to turn. Look at them as confused and hoping that someone will take hold of the operation and get it going again. They're probably all staying out of loyalty to Joe, but how much longer can they go on with small paychecks?''

Vince's "pep" talk was working. For the first time Christy was getting a glimmer of how the men might be feeling. "Confused" couldn't be that far off base, not when she'd been nearly swamped with confusion herself.

What was her real problem with running the job? Wasn't it as simple as not really knowing Joe's crew? Christy thought about it and knew she had just come up against a personal hurdle. She was not ordinarily an aggressive woman. Yes, she'd become more outspoken recently, but she had never in her life deliberately sought positions of authority.

My Lord, she was as bad as Clem, shrinking from unfamiliar responsibility, wishing it would go away, when she knew very well that problems didn't just vanish.

"Thank you," she said softly, and felt her heart gladden at the sight of one of Vince's fabulous smiles.

He'd been watching her, soaking up the pretty picture she made sitting on that stump. Yes, pretty. *Very* pretty. She had beautiful eyes, even clouded as they were with worry. Christy stirred him like no other woman ever had. He could fall very hard for her, he realized, and wondered in the next heartbeat if he hadn't already done so.

One point didn't require clarification—a desire to make love to her. It was clear now that he had felt that gnawing itch the first time they'd talked and that every succeeding meeting had intensified it.

Bending over to reach her, Vince took her by the upper arms and brought her to her feet. Christy's eyes widened. "Vince..." The protest died in her throat when he lifted her to stand on the stump.

"There," he said softly. "This makes us just about the same height."

Their faces were on a level. He had lifted her very easily, proving again how strong he was. His hands rested on her waist, and it felt strange to Christy to be looking straight into his eyes.

A bird fluttered by, followed closely by another, both of them twittering loudly. Other than birdcalls and insect noises, the forest was silent, brilliantly clear and green in the sunshine.

They stood there, Christy on the fat little stump, Vince wearing a very masculine half smile. She studied him, recognizing, as she had that first day in the hospital, that he had a powerful personality and oceans of male confidence. Pursuit was in his blood, his appointed and accepted role in the game between the sexes. If he wanted a woman, he went after her.

And he wanted her, Christy Allen. If she could once believe that it was only because of genuine feelings and had nothing to do with Joe or his contract, she just might...

Christy breathed a small, somewhat dejected sigh. It was really all up to her, wasn't it? The questions and doubts were hers, not Vince's. How strange that such a hurricane of a man should come roaring into her life after so many years of living alone. *And,* thinking that she was contented living alone.

Where was that contentment now? Standing on a stump in the woods to be the same height as a man had a frivolous quality to it. But it was tremendously, profoundly exciting, and right at the moment Christy couldn't find a drop of contentment anywhere in her body. Vince made her feel achy and dissatisfied, as if she was incomplete in some intangible way, as if an important component of life was missing.

"Put your arms around my neck," he instructed softly, taking her hands and moving them to his shoulders. Christy couldn't look away from the hot light in his eyes, and when her hands curled around his shoulders, it suddenly became impossible to breathe at a normal rate.

This wasn't kid stuff. The emotions passing back and forth between them were very adult. His hands slowly moved up and then down her back, from her shoulders to her hips. The question of whether she should be allowing this arose in her mind, appearing very distinct for a few uneasy moments and then receding without resolution.

She was thirty years old and had never been a part of anything so completely sexual. Her feelings for the one man she had supposed herself in love with had been genuine but on a whole different plane than the feelings Vince evoked. But then, she told herself, this wasn't love. This was...what? Lust?

A shiver rippled through her. "Are you cold?" Vince drew her up against himself. "I'll warm you up."

She laid her head on his shoulder, turning her face to his throat. "I'm not cold," she whispered. His hands wouldn't stay still; they kept moving, heating her back, sliding down to her hips. Someone's heartbeat was very loud. Her own? His?

His body was hard, every part of it. And yet it was warm and yielding, a puzzle. He seemed satisfied to just hold her, but she also sensed a deep, inner dissatisfaction in him, another puzzle. However patient he was right now, this tenderness was only a preliminary, a form of foreplay. Perhaps he was lulling her, leading her to think he wasn't really a predator.

His fingertips danced up her spine, and she shuddered with an overwhelming thrill. Involuntarily, it seemed, her lips moved on the side of his throat, and she felt his responsive tensing. Her head was swimming, her knees had nearly stopped supporting her. She was lying against him, relying on his strength to keep her upright.

How very odd—she had energy without strength. Her nerves seemed to be buzzing with animation, and yet her muscles felt as limp as rags. "Vince," she whispered. "We should...do something. Go back to town or...something."

"That's what I'm thinking about—that 'something.'"

His voice had been very low, a husky rumble in his chest and throat. He clasped the back of her head and raised it to see her face. His eyes were dark and intense. "Do you understand what's happening with us?"

A frown flickered across her features, and she searched his eyes for honesty. "Do you?"

He stared, then held her head and slowly, deliberately brought his mouth to hers. Her insides went crazy. His lips moved on hers, opening and devouring hers. It was a kiss of possession, a declaration of intention. A tiny flash of fear darted through her system. They were miles from anyone else, and he was saying very clearly that he intended having her.

But then it all seemed so logical. Didn't she want the same thing? Wasn't she ready for a man with Vince's power? Surely she could sample and not get burned, and besides, doubts about her mistrust of this man were beginning to pile up. No one could convey the kind of sincerity he did with only deceit in his soul, no one!

Christy's mouth began to move in a kiss of her own, opening, participating, and she rubbed against him, her breasts on his chest, her thighs on his lower body. His arms tightened around her, squeezing her closer. The kissing went on...and on...with only brief interruptions for air. She was weak from the kissing, sapped from the onslaught of a truly aroused male dedicated to only one conclusion.

His hands began to wander again, seeking bare skin this time, lifting the hem of her outer shirt and burrowing beneath her inner. "You've got on an awful lot of clothes," he mumbled raggedly.

"Because of the fog . . . and the sunshine."

"Are you warm enough now?"

"I'm . . . very warm," she breathed.

"Then let's get rid of one of these shirts."

The offending garment seemed to disappear from her body, and then he was unbuttoning the other shirt. She dampened her lips and watched him doing it, looking down at his big fingers working the buttons loose. "Maybe I'm not *that* warm," she whispered huskily, a wan objection to losing all of her clothing.

"We'll leave it on. I just want to see you."

"Oh." She tried to remember which bra she had put on that morning and hoped it was one of her prettier ones.

Actually, it didn't matter, because he paid absolutely no attention to it. In fact, it was unhooked and pushed out of the way so quickly she might as well have been braless.

And then he was looking at her naked breasts, wearing an aching, yearning expression. "You're very beautiful," he whispered hoarsely.

Was she? With Vince's gaze warming her skin, she felt beautiful. Flushed and tingly and proud to be a woman. He wasn't lying or pretending. He wasn't!

His hands cupped her breasts, holding them, lifting them, caressing them. She put her head back and closed her eyes, reveling in the heated sensation. And then she felt his mouth, his tongue and lips on a nipple, wetting it, sucking on it, all done so very gently, as though he wasn't a rough-hewn man at all. There was nothing to fear from Vince just because they were out here alone, she realized dizzily, and if she was looking for a reason to fear something, she had better look to herself. Never before in her life had she been led solely by her senses, and that was exactly what was happening right now.

She could very easily shed the rest of her clothing, stand here on this stump and let him touch her naked body anywhere he chose. He would kiss her all over, he would moisten her skin with his tongue, he would rub and tease and taste, and it would be the most gloriously wanton experience of her life.

Faint, moaning noises were coming out of her throat. "Christy, honey," he whispered thickly, so hot and worked up that he was in pain. This was no place to be making this kind of love, although he was nearly to the point of no return. He shouldn't have started things out here. He should have waited until they got back to town. Only human, he was crass enough to understand the advantage of good timing, and this wasn't even close. And yet they were both so ready. She wasn't an easy woman and, he suspected, her present, almost dreamlike passion was unusual.

He felt so tender toward her. Along with a desperate desire he felt tenderness, a potent combination of emotions. Falling for her? Yeah, that was exactly what was happening.

"Christy," he whispered, raising his head and pressing his lips to the pulse in her throat.

"Hmm?"

"Let's go to my place."

A ray of reality seeped through the feverish daze of Christy's mind. That was what Vince had requested before, too—to go to his place. Did she dare? Her own body was saying, *Yes, do it. Go with him. Do whatever he asks.*

But what would people say if it got around Rock Falls? Laura would never be against her daughter having a relationship with a man, probably not any man if he was a decent sort. But what about Joe? Would he mutter some gruff remark about fraternizing with the enemy?

Christy looked at the big man holding her and touched his face with a gently testing forefinger. A woman couldn't resent a man for being male and certainly not for defining her own femaleness. Especially when she was a willing partner to his advances. Her shirt was open and her bra was askew, but disarray and near-nudity wasn't bothering her nearly as much as what she saw in Vince's eyes. He wanted nothing else to matter to her and knew that so much did, and there was something sad about outside factors influencing a relationship.

She sighed, a long intake and release of breath that told Vince her mood was changing. Which he had feared would happen if he gave her the chance to think. Not that he normally relied on pressure with women. But Christy seemed to be so overwhelmed by everything going on, and she'd forgotten it all for a few incredibly beautiful minutes.

It was over for now, though. She was remembering again, thinking about responsibility and loyalty and who he was and who she was. She smiled softly, remorsefully, and holding his hand for support, stepped down off of the stump. Then she turned her back to him and adjusted her clothing.

Vince cursed under his breath, his lips grim, his eyes glittering with frustration. He walked away, needing a minute or two to cool down. Christy was right about one thing: they were in one hell of a crazy situation—Joe laid up, her worried about this logging job, that stupid damn feud between the two companies. And, yes, he knew her suspicions about Joe's contract.

If only there was something he could do to help out more effectively. Pep talks were fine, and deep down he knew Christy could do the job. Anyone could who understood the basics of the business and was willing to put out the effort. Christy's biggest liability was her own lack of confidence.

But it grated to have to admit just how tightly his hands were tied beyond doling out advice. Morrison men wouldn't work for a Bonnell, and Vince knew if the roles were reversed, his own men wouldn't work for Joe. It was all so foolish, but until now he'd only seen the fistfights and pranks as funny.

In his present mood *nothing* seemed funny.

Their conversation was rather stilted and wrapped around a good many long smoldering looks, but Vince and Christy walked among the equipment while he thoroughly explained each piece's function. She listened and made notes, gratefully adding Vince's information to what she already knew about the bulldozers, the lines and grapples, the boom loader and every other piece of machinery in the clearing and woods.

The sawyers owned and maintained their own power saws, but they were the only employees who didn't operate company equipment.

"Set a daily production figure," Vince instructed. "From past records you know what this crew is capable of delivering. Harp on that figure, insist upon it. You can bet Joe does that. Eight loads, ten, twelve, whatever makes a good day, set that goal and push the men into hitting it. Every single workday.

"One thing to watch for are overly eager sawyers. They get paid by the thousand board feet they cut, and sometimes get a little carried away without supervision. Without one single log having been trucked to the mill, you can end up owing them a large sum of money on payday."

Christy nodded, recalling a few such incidents even under Joe's sharp eye. Actually, very little Vince was telling her was completely alien. Throughout the years and without really trying she had absorbed an incredible amount of information about the physical end of the business. Only, until today she hadn't realized how much she did know.

In the long run the day wasn't wasted time. Christy recognized her own knowledge now and the fact that her biggest hang-up was with personalities—definitely positive gains. At least on Monday she wouldn't feel like such an amateur, she decided.

When every subject seemed to be exhausted, they started walking back to Vince's pickup. "Thank you," she said with genuine appreciation.

Vince opened the passenger door for her. "You're welcome." He glanced at his watch during the brief trip around the front of the pickup. They had been out here for a long time, but it was still only a quarter to one, hours away from the dinner he had planned for the two of them at his house this evening.

He drove slowly, stretching the miles back to where Christy had left Joe's truck. "Do you have plans for this afternoon?" he finally asked.

"I'll probably drop in on Joe, and if I'm going to be in the woods next week, there's some bookwork to bring up to date." Keeping both jobs on-line would require long workdays, she thought with a slight frown. But that would be a small price to pay if she succeeded. And she had to succeed; failure had too many horrifying ramifications. What would Joe do without his business? It wasn't a matter of money. His equipment had an impressive value and could be sold for enough cash, even after paying off bank loans, to see him through the rest of his life and then some.

But there was a lot more to a happy life than money, and Joe's heart and soul were interwoven into his company. He wasn't a sitter, a reader or a television watcher. He had no hobbies, no avocation that would occupy a man who had enjoyably filled his sixty-odd years with work.

Joe was a rough-hewn man, too, very much like Vince. The Oregon woods seemed to produce men of the earth—strong, rugged individuals who preferred work over hobbies. But then it also produced men like Stubb, who drank too much, and Clem, who worked hard but couldn't face responsibility.

For some reason Christy felt more in tune with the area and its residents. "I'm seeing things a little differently," she murmured.

"Pardon?" Vince was still contemplating dinner together, wondering how to get from one o'clock to six without losing Christy's attention.

She turned in the seat to face him. "I grew up in Rock Falls, and only now am I beginning to understand it."

"You moved away."

"For six years."

He sent her a glance. "Was there ever anyone important, Christy?"

Did their pasts need discussion? Something was happening between her and Vince. There was no longer a question in her mind about the sincerity of his desire. Christy felt his wanting right now, and just looking at him had the power to raise her blood pressure. He filled his side of the pickup, and she was beginning to equate size with sensuality, thick, dark, unruly hair and gray eyes with eroticism.

But there was more. In a man big and strong enough to wrestle alligators, there was a tremendous capacity for tenderness. She felt affection mixed in with his desire, so it wasn't all lust.

"There was a man once," she finally replied quietly. "We planned to be married. He backed out at the last minute."

Vince shot her a sharp glance. The episode had hurt her and was probably the reason she stuck so much to herself. Vince's stomach tightened with jealousy, surprising him in its intensity. "The man...what happened to him after that?"

Christy stared. Was he truly interested? Concerned? Curiosity about her past love life seemed so alien to Vince's confident personality, but the need to know was on his face and in his voice. "Vince," she said softly. "It's been over for a long time."

A sudden urge struck Christy. If Vince wanted to hear details, there were a few that might make him sit up and take notice. "He was a deceitful man. I ignored the signs and lived to regret it. But I vowed never again to get involved with a man I didn't trust immediately and implicitly."

Vince sucked in a jagged breath. Christy's point was arrow-straight and piercing. He got it, all right, and understood her reluctance a whole hell of a lot better. "You're a complex woman."

"Isn't everyone? In varying ways, of course. But we're all products of experience, Vince." You, too, she implied.

He cleared his throat. "Is that when you moved back to Rock Falls?"

"No. I had a reasonably good job in Seattle, but during a week at home with Mother and Joe, I learned that he'd been without good office help for several months. The place was a disaster. Joe couldn't find anything and his records were in a mess. I volunteered to move back and take over his office." Christy sighed. "Joe's a very special man, Vince."

"Everyone's special in their own way."

"Yes, but some people's ways are... well, irritating. Or offensive."

Vince smiled. "True. Anyway, you mentioned seeing things differently."

"Yes. I've kept pretty much to myself, staying out of local affairs. I know a lot of people, of course, but not very well. My own doing."

"Why?"

"Because..." She had to think about it and still didn't have a logical explanation. "I'm not sure. I've never sought bright lights, anyway, and maybe I just dropped out."

That theory sounded plausible. Vince knew she'd been around town for years, but she'd never been a real part of it. Not that everyone was involved in every social or civic activity. As in most towns, Rock Falls had a mixture of doers and citizens with few interests beyond their own families. But even habitual stay-at-homers were more visible than Christy had been.

She was coming out of her shell, Vince suspected, which pleased him. With Christy it seemed that one step at a time was wise, and maybe he'd been rushing her. Oddly he too felt rushed. They were being swept along by circumstance, him as well as her. And he couldn't pretend not to want her.

Reaching their original point, Vince parked his pickup next to Joe's. He looked at his passenger. "Dinner tonight, Christy?"

Her gaze washed over his features. There were no smiles on his face, not on his lips, not in his eyes, and he was a man

who smiled often. His serious mood moved Christy, but she
was back on track again. "I can't go to your house, Vince,"
she said gently. "Maybe... sometime, but not tonight."

She wasn't slamming the door, merely decreasing the
breadth of its opening. And he couldn't even question her
reasons, not when he knew them all so well now.

The corner of his mouth turned up, just a tiny little re-
laxation of tension. She was an honest, guileless woman,
unashamed of passion but unswayed from more noble pur-
suits by its lure. And trust was profoundly important to her.
In this case trust might take a little time. She hadn't "immediately and implicitly" put her faith in Vince Bonnell's
offer of assistance.

Christy's mouth twitched, a shadow of a smile in response to his, and she reached for the door handle. "Thank
you for today."

"Anytime. I'll call."

"Yes... fine."

A minute later Vince watched her drive off. All in all, it
had been quite a day. There was room for disappointment,
but something solid was growing between him and Christy.
Her objections to him were scaling away. In time everything would fall into place.

And all he had to do was practice patience. He grinned
wryly. Patience wasn't one of his strong suits.

Eight

Christy filled Saturday afternoon exactly as she'd told Vince—with a visit to the hospital and then hours at her desk and computer. Periodically she dialed Clem's home telephone number, which he finally answered around five. Her explanation was brief and to the point. "I'll be out at the job site on Monday morning, Clem. Until Stubb gets back I'll be overseeing the operation. Would you please let the other men know?"

The long silence in Christy's ear conveyed Clem's surprise. But the reaction wasn't unexpected, and she gave Clem as much time as he needed to digest the news. Finally the old logger made a gruff reply. "Well, I guess that'll be all right. Never worked for a woman before, though."

"I'm sure we'll get along. May I rely on you to spread the word?"

"You think you can handle it, huh?"

"Yes, I think I can." She sounded positive, which was what she had intended. Her remaining doubts about her own ability, or lack thereof, were going to be kept to herself. Besides, how much worse could things get in the woods? Her supervision wouldn't be any laxer than Clem's, and it just might be a whole lot better.

"Well...I'll make a few phone calls. See you on Monday."

"Thank you, Clem."

The connection was broken without a "goodbye," and shaking her head at the old man's curtness, Christy put the phone down. The wheels were in motion; Joe's crew would soon know that she was taking over. Despite Vince's opinion that the men would "bust their britches" to work for her, she didn't expect total nor united cooperation. There was bound to be some resistance, but she could only hope no one would object to her involvement to the point of quitting his job.

Christy turned back to the computer. She wanted all the records up-to-date before Monday morning so she could fully focus on the job at hand. She had already told her mother that she had some things to catch up on at the office and wouldn't be having dinner with her, so there was no reason to watch the clock.

At nine-thirty she rubbed her tired eyes, turned off the computer and left the office. After stopping at a drive-in for a chicken sandwich to go, she drove home. She fed Muffin, ate the sandwich with a glass of milk, took a shower and crawled into bed, positive she would go out like a light.

She didn't, though. All afternoon she'd been aware of Vince in the back of her mind, but her work had kept her seriously occupied. Now there was no computer flashing demands at her, and in her dark and quiet bedroom the man was almost real enough to touch.

She knew she would never again be the same woman she'd been before Joe's accident. Every meeting with Vince, every touch, every kiss, every single factor of their peculiar relationship strongly affected her. Lying in bed, she realized just how lonely she really was. She didn't have to be. She could pick up the phone right now, and every cell in her body told her that Vince would come over and be thrilled to share this solitary bed. With only a few words into that telephone she could spend the night in Vince's arms and feel everything and more of what she had felt with him today.

Christy sighed uneasily. She wasn't a person who regarded risk-taking with any degree of fondness. Even though she was becoming more alert to life's possibilities, she would never deliberately go out and seek the unfamiliar, the unknown.

But she might seek Vince's brand of excitement. Thinking of the morning and his kisses made her feel achy again, empty, very alone. Her personality had taken an abrupt change since meeting Vince. She thought about sex a lot. And fulfillment, which she was living without, about feelings and emotions, and about how Vince might react to an affair.

He had never been married, which could mean any number of things. Did he purposely avoid serious commitment, or had marriage merely eluded him?

Was he as surprised by their passionate need of each other as she was, or was this kind of hunger only routine for him?

And finally, would analysis or knowledge or anything else prevent her from making love with Vince?

Her heartbeat clamored in her ears. She was on the verge of doing something that she could only pray wouldn't hurt other people. She was moving against the tide, swimming upstream, and she'd never felt so pulled before. She grasped at Vince's good points, attempting to rationalize her own weakness, to make it acceptable.

He did have good points, she told herself. The overconfidence that had initially raised her guard was really a plus, she told herself. He was kindhearted...and generous... and his sense of humor was to be admired...and...

And he was Vincent Bonnell and she was Joe Morrison's stepdaughter.

Christy finally drifted off to sleep, but it was with tears glistening beneath her eyes.

Sunday consisted of attending church, a visit to the hospital and more hours at the computer. By four that afternoon Christy had every phase of her accounting system current. With a sense of satisfaction she shut the computer down, cleared her desk of all remnants of work and then stood up and stretched her back.

Between church and the hospital she had gone home and changed from a good dress into something more casual. Because the sun was out and warm today she had put on a cotton skirt and blouse, and sandals. Maybe summer had finally arrived, she hoped, although the advancing calendar didn't guarantee clear skies on the Oregon coast.

She looked around the office. One more chore should be done before she returned to the hospital and dinner with her mother—some cleaning. Nothing major, but the floor needed vacuuming and a little dusting was in order.

The dusting was taken care of in a very few minutes, then she got out the vacuum cleaner. It was an old thing with a noisy motor that obliterated all other sounds. Christy moved quickly, pushing the machine into corners and under her desk.

She turned it toward the door and felt her stomach take a sudden drop. Vince was leaning against the casing with his arms folded across his chest. His rugged good looks and powerful masculinity struck her right between the eyes, and he wasn't smiling.

She switched off the vacuum, and the motor died a wheezing death. "How long have you been standing there?"

"A few minutes."

He looked purposeful, and instinct told her why he'd come. Her mouth seemed suddenly dryer. Her words were hasty and stumbling over one another. "I've been trying to get everything ready for tomorrow. It would bother me to leave the office in a mess."

"You don't like loose ends."

"Something like that."

"I decided to come by rather than call."

"Apparently."

"Do you mind?"

Her heart was beating too hard and she wasn't breathing easily. His gaze was wandering, taking in her bare legs below the hem of her skirt. She noted his low-riding jeans and white shirt, and the magnificent body they covered, the massive shoulders, the heavily muscled thighs, the curvature of maleness below his worn leather belt.

Even if that foolish old feud had been a life-and-death struggle, she would want Vince Bonnell. Last night's traumatic effect was still with her. Her night had been restive, full of fretful dreams. From the look on his face he hadn't gotten much rest, either.

"No, I don't mind," she admitted huskily.

"You worked late last night."

She unplugged the vacuum and got very busy winding the cord. "Yes."

"I drove by and almost stopped. I was only going to drive by again, but...here I am."

Christy pushed the vacuum to the closet, put it away and closed the closet door. "Everything's in good shape in here now."

"I'd say so."

He wasn't talking about the office. If he did what she suspected he'd come for, she wouldn't stop him. Her resistance to his potency had gradually been deserting her, and now it just didn't seem to exist at all. Yesterday's events at the logging site and then feeling so alone last night had finished depleting her defenses.

Christy dampened her lips when Vince reached behind himself and snapped the dead bolt on the door. "So we won't be disturbed," he said softly.

Her mind darted around the two-room office. Joe's office contained a couch, but it certainly wasn't big enough to accommodate Vince. And yet his expression said he was going to test her again, take her to the limits of her own sensibility. She could always say no; she knew that now with Vince. But she wasn't going to say no, and she wondered how they would manage.

Her eyes went to the windows, which were adorned with half-opened miniblinds. The tension in the room was almost palpable, making her entire body tingle. Vince went to each window and adjusted the slats of the blinds, moving unhurriedly, taking his time. He had hoped for a positive reception, having put in one hell of a frustrated night. He'd stopped by to check Christy's mood, and it was elating to realize she'd driven back to town yesterday as frustrated as him.

He was picking up strong, arousing vibes from her. Responsibility and loyalty were no longer the only important things in her life. She'd faced her own sensuality and found something lacking. Vince took a deep breath and turned away from the last window. She was standing near her desk, a beautiful, sexy woman, waiting for him. For *him!*

His pulse went wild. He held his rushing emotions in check and slowly walked over to her. In low-heeled sandals she was so small that he felt like a giant. He had always preferred bigger women, but this little person was beginning to mean more to him than any woman ever had. The top of her hair was level with his shirt pocket, and she had to tilt her head back to see his face. He threaded his fingers into her hair. "I love your hair loose like this."

"It's the way I usually wear it."

"That day in the hospital, the first time we talked, I wanted to do this." Both of his hands played in her hair.

She was staring. "You're so big, Vince."

"I don't scare you, do I?"

She found a weak smile. "No."

"Good." His hands dropped to her waist, and he lifted her slowly, raising her up off of the floor. She slid her hands around to the back of his head and locked them together.

Their lips met in a brief, almost tentative kiss. They looked at each other. "You're not going to stop me, are you?" he whispered, amazed delight in his eyes.

"I...can't."

"Oh, honey." He brought her closer, wrapping his arms around her, molding her body to his. His kiss was deep, hot and thorough, and he held her as though he would never let her go.

Christy sighed with an immediate flow of emotions, giving him everything his lips and arms and body asked for. Reality was quickly giving way to fantasy, and her power to deny the heady sensation was too pitiful to draw upon.

She kissed him back, with just as much fervor as he was kissing her. Her mouth opened and nestled into his, stroking and caressing while their tongues touched, danced, mated.

A growl of pleasure built in his throat. In hers, too. The embrace had a primal, lusty feel. Nothing beyond this little office building had any meaning for either of them. Of their own volition, it seemed, her legs rose and clamped around him.

"That's it," he whispered, his lips moving on hers, then settling into another wildly consuming kiss.

She had never been attracted to a really big man before, and Vince's size was part of his appeal. Why it would matter eluded Christy, but she knew it did. He made her feel completely feminine, and powerful in a strange way. Maybe the sense of power came out of arousing a man twice her size. She did like the way he was able to lift and hold her, she knew with every certainty.

Her interior felt like liquid fire and nearly as unstable, darting one way and then another, turning her bones to jelly, making her feel soft and loose-jointed.

Vince sat her on the desk and had to bend over to sustain another kiss. Christy felt herself being gently but insistently pushed backward while he kissed her breathless. There was no haste in his movements. As worked up as she was and knew he was, it took what felt like an eternity of kisses to bring her to her back. She was lying on her own desk, a piece of utilitarian furniture she would never be dispassionate about again.

And then, with the brush of one hand, Vince swept away the few items that hadn't been tucked into drawers—a cup of pens and pencils, a small calendar. They tumbled to the floor, and Christy's heart expanded with exhilaration, with sexual energy. She laughed, a husky, throaty ripple made of pure joy.

Vince raised his head and saw the untamed sensuousness on her face, the exultation. His smile crinkled the corners of his eyes. They might be miles apart in other areas—and he wasn't altogether positive of that anymore—but they couldn't be any closer emotionally than they were at this moment. It was an intoxicating feeling, a rare feeling.

The heels of her sandals hooked onto the edge of the desk, her knees angled and pointing upward, one on either side of him. He leaned over her, cradled in the V of her thighs. "I could fall in love with you," he whispered.

Her eyes were full of seductive mischief. "It seems very possible right now, doesn't it?"

"Very." His gaze adored her, feature by feature. Her hair was a silken pillow beneath her head, and he touched it, marveling again at its unique texture. Then he straightened up and began unbuttoning his shirt.

Christy watched him remove it. The bronzed skin on his wide chest was split by a patch of black hair. His belly was flat and firm. He was utterly male, utterly beautiful.

Folding the shirt, Vince bent forward again, lifted her head and laid the garment down for a pillow. His hands moved to the buttons on her blouse, working each one open. He smiled when he saw the clasp at the front of her bra, and flicked it open, too.

His smile faded, his expression evolving into adoration. He breathed through his mouth, his chest rising and falling, while he touched her breasts. Her nipples stood upright and rigid for him, and her thighs flexed, tightening, holding him. He dipped his head and took one puckered bud into his mouth. With a little moan Christy twined her hands into his hair.

He sucked gently, with his tongue teasing. His right hand worked its way downward, going under her skirt, stopping at the silky barrier of her panties. "Wait," she hoarsely whispered, and urged him to step back.

There was no other way. Silent except for his heavy breathing, Vince moved away, closed her legs and slid her panties down. She expected him to take up his previous position immediately and relaxed her thighs again to give him room. Only he had another idea, one that widened her eyes and stole her breath.

He was looking at her in the most intimate way possible, and doing it boldly with erotic pleasure on his face. She trembled and tried to close her quivering thighs. He shook his head. "No. Let me see you."

She was breathing hard. Making love meant different things to different people, but no one had ever done this to her before. Not quite like this. Not with such voluptuous pleasure, not with such fiery curiosity.

She jumped when he touched her but couldn't seem to tell him to stop. His hands splayed on her inner thighs, stroking their softness, and she had never seen so much passion in a man's eyes. Her heart was hammering, pounding against her rib cage. "Vince..."

He bent over and pressed his mouth to a thigh, but one kiss wasn't all he wanted. His lips moved upward, shocking her. He wasn't going to...?

But he was going to, and he did, and she nearly fainted at the hot surge of pleasure such intimacy delivered. She had read about this in novels, but this particular aspect of lovemaking had completely eluded her personal experience.

His tongue...his mouth...so hot...so wet. "Vince," she moaned on a sob, knowing she was fighting a losing battle with sensibility. How did he know so much about a woman?

How did he know exactly which spot to tease and tantalize? She was so hot that she was sweating, and she never sweated.

But then she was doing a lot of things she'd never done before.

Her head moved back and forth on the shirt-pillow. She was flushed and dazed, her small whimpers increasing to cries of unrestrained gratification. Wantonness snuck up on her, and the yearning in her body was reaching an end, coming to a glorious conclusion.

Vince stood and unbuckled his belt. His eyes were dark and untamed-looking. He watched Christy while he got a small packet out of his pocket, then he unzipped his fly.

She stared, unable to do anything else. She was emotionally disabled, hanging on the edge of a cliff. Her face was flushed and damp, her swollen lips parted, her breasts nude, her skirt tangled around her waist.

She couldn't think. The wanting, the needing, was consuming her. Vince shoved his jeans and undershorts down. Without turning away he took care of protection, mesmerizing Christy with the simple process.

Then he moved between her thighs again and bent forward to kiss her mouth. Her system spun out of control. Holding this naked giant of a man, she wept while he kissed her and whispered how beautiful she was. And then she felt his penetration and sobbed into his shoulder while he slid deeply into her body.

He moved slowly, in and out, again and again, and he supported his weight on his elbows on the desk, one on either side of her head. "Open your eyes," he whispered. "Look at me."

Tears blurred her vision when she complied. The heat in her lower body was almost painful. She was riding the crest, on the verge of going over. She hadn't expected so much. She'd admitted desire, she'd faced her own need, but she hadn't expected the mind-shattering force of Vince's power.

He began to move faster, with more demand in his thrusts. "Let yourself go," he commanded.

And then it commenced, the final, explosive rush to completion. He was sweating, too, determined to last until she was ready. Her cries were signals, and when they became gasping, and her fingernails began digging into his back, he knew it was time.

He gave in to the pressure of his own body and rode her without gentleness. He felt her spasms before his own, heard her final cry before his, and the intensity of his release was so pleasurable that he nearly blacked out.

He tried not to collapse on her, but his body was trembling and weak. He lay there for a moment, catching his breath. She was small and soft beneath him, breathing in shuddering sobs.

Raising his head, he looked at her. Her eyes were teary, her lips parted. "Why did you cry?"

"I...don't know. It was so..."

He smiled tenderly. "Yes, it was. But then we both knew it would be, didn't we?"

She nodded, a hint of helplessness in the gesture.

"You're wonderful," he said, giving her a long, probing look. "Small and perfect. I didn't hurt you, did I?"

The negative shake of her head also contained that hint of helplessness. She was still dazed, physically replete but a little staggered by the intensity of the passion they had just shared.

He kissed her lips, lingering on their sweetness. Then he smiled. "Where's the bathroom?"

She raised a limp hand and pointed. "Over there."

He left her body, reached down and yanked up his jeans and shorts and went into the bathroom, closing the door behind him.

She lay there just as he'd left her for several moments and then moved her legs. Her thighs ached, her back, too. Slowly and carefully she pulled herself up. A very few minutes ago she'd noticed no discomfort whatsoever. Now she

knew that she would feel the results of making love on a
desk for days.

Straightening her bra, she reclasped it and began button-
ing her blouse. She slid off the desk and found her panties.
The bathroom door opened, and she quickly slipped the
panties into her skirt pocket.

Vince was put back together. His jeans were zipped and
belted. Instead of going to the desk for his wadded-up shirt,
he went over to her and put his arms around her. She sighed
and rested her cheek on his chest, noticing the tickle of the
bristly hair there.

"How about dinner together tonight?" he asked, putting some humor into the question, implying that they might
not have eaten together last night, but what could possibly
get in the way of doing so tonight?

Christy felt herself melting against him and wondered
how she could feel anything even remotely sexual after the
incredible satisfaction she had just experienced.

It was happening to Vince, too, and he grinned about it.
Just as he'd suspected, once wasn't going to be enough with
Christy. As he'd admitted to himself several times and to her
while they were making love, he was probably falling head
over heels for her.

"Come to my place or invite me to yours," he told her,
moving his face in her hair, breathing in its clean scent.

"I promised Mom..."

"You can call the hospital and beg off."

"Yes, but—"

He raised her chin and looked down at her. "Are you
feeling regret?"

Was she? Maybe what scared her was that her satisfaction, which had felt so permanent, was already being
threatened. In the circle of Vince's arms, up against his hard
form, she was again responding. And it was so soon, and
extremely disturbing.

He let go of her hand to run his hand down her body, following the female curves of breast, waist and hip. "Don't be sorry," he whispered.

She felt him drawing her skirt up, bunching it, reaching its hem. He sucked in a sharp breath when he encountered bare skin, and then caressed the smooth, rounded contours of her hips.

His touch was pure magic, and she thought of what the evening together could bring.

"We could make love in a bed," he whispered. "I want to see your hair spread out on a pillow. Christy, this isn't just a passing fancy with us. You do know that, don't you?"

Her eyes linked with his. "Yes, I guess I do."

He searched the gray-green depths before him. "But you're worrying again. I hope it's not about me."

"You're part of it." She pulled away from him and put a little space between them. "You're something brand-new to me," she admitted almost sadly. "Without everything else going on I'd probably do anything you asked."

His eyes glittered devilishly. "And you'd walk around with a smile on your face. I guarantee it."

"I don't doubt it," she replied evenly. "But you and I aren't the only players, are we? I've got a lot of other things to think about, a lot to do."

He moved to the desk and touched its surface almost affectionately. "Do you think I'm going to leave you alone after this? No way."

Leaving the desk, he walked back over to her and put his hands on her shoulders. "We're a couple, Christy. It might sound overbearing to call you my woman, but that's how I feel. And I'm your man."

She swallowed and dampened her lips. "You're talking about . . . fidelity?"

"I'm talking about spending time together, about getting to really know each other, about finding out just what we do have together."

"And about making love," she whispered, deeply moved by his urge to commit.

"Ah, yes, lots and lots of lovemaking. Starting tonight."

"I think we've *already* started," she replied with some wryness.

She received a completely masculine grin, one brimming with pride and possessiveness. Wherever they went from here, he would never regret today, she realized. Any small feelings of regret *she* had were silly and immature. She had wanted and almost asked for what he had given her. Maybe not in the exact terms in which he had performed, but he was just more experienced than she was and a whole lot bolder.

Nevertheless, she couldn't devote herself to Vince right now. Her time and energies were already committed. There wasn't room in her life for a torrid, time-consuming love affair. And that was what it would be. With Vince it had to be all or nothing, and that was her own instinct, not his.

Christy took a big breath. "Vince, I want—*need*—some time."

"Time?"

"Yes." Christy's hands came up, a placating gesture. Her expression was unabashedly hopeful. "Give me—" she paused to think "—a few weeks." Yes, she thought. She should have better control of the business in a few weeks.

"Time," Vince repeated soberly. Living without her for the next two weeks wasn't in his plans. Not after today. This lady was in his blood, and he'd been envisioning some very exciting nights for the two of them.

Then he saw the determined gleam in her eyes. "You're serious."

"I *have* to be serious." She began pacing. "I'm not going to let this business go down the drain. You probably don't understand, but Joe's been like my own father. He's wonderful to Mom, and he's always been there for me."

She stopped to face him. "Vince, I know there's something important... What I mean is, I'm not trying to ignore... or devalue..."

"Us?" he asked softly. He was thinking about what she was requesting and knew it was only because of Joe and the business. He couldn't be selfish with her now, although he had little doubt that he could pressure her into a commitment to him.

He relaxed into a smile. "All right. I understand."

"You do?" Her tension changed to elation. "Thank you."

Vince took her into his arms and kissed her. "We'll do whatever it takes, okay?"

They were kissing again when the telephone rang. Murmuring a husky "Excuse me," Christy slipped from Vince's arms and picked up the phone. "Morrison Logging Company."

"Christy? Are you still working, honey?"

"Oh, Mom. I'm sorry I'm so late. I'll be at the hospital in..." She needed a shower before she met Laura for dinner. "I'll be there in about forty minutes, Mom."

Vince walked her out to her car and grinned as he helped her into it. "My pickup's been out here for quite a while, Christy."

She nibbled her bottom lip thoughtfully. "Maybe I can't worry about gossip anymore."

His smile broadened. "Good. I'll give you all the room you need for two weeks, Christy, but not a day more."

She nodded gratefully. "If I don't have things worked out by then, I probably never will."

"You'll manage."

"I wish I were as confident of that as you are."

Nine

"**J**oe seems to be doing well today," Christy commented while scanning Mabel's familiar menu.

Laura glanced up. "Yes, I thought so."

Christy wasn't even close to being hungry, although she hadn't eaten anything since breakfast. But the awareness of what she had done this afternoon seemed to be filling her entire system, including her stomach. Deciding on a turkey sandwich, Christy closed the menu. "He doesn't seem very interested in the business, Mom. Have you noticed?"

"I think he's only interested in getting well enough to go home," Laura said with a warm, indulgent smile.

"Has Dr. Martin mentioned how long Joe will have to remain in the hospital?"

Laura nodded. "About another two weeks, barring any complications."

"Two weeks" was becoming a milestone in more ways than one. Putting Vince on hold was only sensible right now, but there was more to consider about that incredible hour than a seemingly wise decision. She had behaved completely out of character today, and yes, there was a streak of regret in her system. Did she trust Vince now? She certainly felt something for him—a whole lot of something if she were to be totally honest. But what did the occurrence on her desk have to do with trust?

Lord, they should have waited, Christy thought in a wave of almost crippling weakness. Delaying intimacy never harmed a solid liaison, and leaping headlong into a physical relationship wasn't at all like her. As usual, away from Vince's strong influence, everything looked different. It had been so easy to tell him she wasn't going to worry about gossip anymore, and it wasn't even remotely true. Of course gossip could hurt her.

No, not her. Joe. He couldn't possibly be unperturbed should he hear that she and Vince Bonnell were becoming an item.

Christy sighed inwardly. She had stuck her neck out and would have to face any resulting consequences. But she was profoundly relieved about that two-week respite—*if* Vince kept his word about it, that is. There was that term popping up again: trust. As things stood right now between her and Vince, she had no choice but to trust that he would give her the room he'd promised.

In the meantime she had a business to run. She cleared her throat. "I've got something to tell you, Mom."

"Go right ahead."

Christy met her mother's soft brown eyes across the table. She hadn't once hinted that things could be better with the business. In fact, the entire subject had been discussed in only the most general terms since Joe's accident. But Christy knew that she couldn't go out to the woods every day without forewarning Laura.

"I've decided to do Joe's job in the woods," she stated calmly.

Laura stared. "I'm afraid I don't understand."

How best to put this? "There's...a problem with supervision. Clem Molinski attempted the job, but he didn't work out. There's no one else."

"And *you're* going to try it? Christy, that's no job for a woman!"

Her mother was aghast, which Christy had predicted would be the case. "It's not a matter of choice, Mom," she said gently.

"But Joe employs more than a dozen men. Surely one of them can..." Laura's voice trailed off. "I'm sure you've thought it through, but I don't want you in the woods. You'll get hurt."

Christy smiled and pointed out, "Joe's only injury in forty years of logging happened at his own home, Mom, not in the woods."

Laura remained unconvinced. "Do you even know what has to be done out there?"

"I've got a pretty good idea. I really don't want you worrying about it, Mom. I only told you so you would know where I'll be during the day. The mornings, especially. I'm going to try to get back to the office by early afternoon so I can keep things going there, too."

Laura looked on the verge of tears. "This is awful. When I tell Joe—"

"No!" Christy leaned forward. "Promise me you won't say anything to Joe about it. He doesn't need to know, Mom."

Sighing dejectedly, Laura relented. "No, I suppose he doesn't. He'd only worry, and what good would that do?"

"Exactly."

A few minutes after Christy turned off the bedroom lamp that night the headlights of a slowly moving vehicle illuminated the room. She thought of Vince immediately and stiffened, relaxing only when the car passed on by. She didn't want to live the next two weeks on the edge, always wondering if every car driving by was Vince, but would she be able to stop herself?

Her feelings weren't familiar anymore, Christy admitted uneasily. She was accustomed to a bland existence, and today's high-voltage lovemaking had shocked her onto a whole other plane. Was she falling in love with Vince?

Was it love they were *both* dealing with? He'd mentioned love, so he was speculating, too. Love, to Christy, denoted permanence. When a man and woman fell in love with each other, marriage followed. And babies, and growing old together. It was what she'd thought she had found one other time in her life.

She was still single, so love, marriage and babies were not as simple as one, two, three. Christy shuddered. She didn't want another bout of pain, not like she'd gone through before. What flaw in her personality drew her to men who *could* hurt her?

With Vince everything was so physical. She got all feverish just thinking about their activities on her desk. Vince obviously had a fertile imagination and the courage to follow through. His big, beautiful body, naked, hot, aroused, was etched in her mind. He'd taken her to unsuspected heights of fulfillment. But dare she construe raw, perfect sexuality as love?

Christy thought of tall, handsome sons and daughters and attempted to reconcile a future with Vince. Someday everything would be back to normal. Joe would be well and functioning again. She would be only a bookkeeper again. But how would she ever get Joe and Vince together?

She sighed helplessly, then turned over, forced her eyes shut and told herself to go to sleep. Four in the morning was an ungodly time to have to haul oneself out of bed, and if she didn't get some sleep, tomorrow would be worse than she already feared.

The day began with Christy's alarm clock buzzing raucously and startling her out of a sound sleep. She threw back the covers and headed for the shower, the best way she knew of to wake up two hours before she normally did.

Breakfast, feeding Muffin and dressing for the woods took up a half hour. Christy hurriedly packed a sack lunch. The men started working at six, and she wanted to be there when they arrived.

Her nerves were as jagged as broken glass. She dashed from one thing to another and finally left the house at ten minutes to five. The air was cool, the sky cloudy. It looked like rain again. She threw her lunch, hard hat and rain jacket onto the seat of Joe's pickup and climbed up behind the wheel.

During the drive, she thought about Stubb and wondered again—with resentment, with rancor—just what it was that he was doing. If it was all up to her, when he did get back she would fire him on the spot. How would Joe handle such carelessness? She'd been remiss in not telling Stubb about the situation when he called, but the man was totally undependable. How could she have suspected he might not come home immediately?

Live and learn, she thought grimly, then expanded the conclusive thought. She was living and learning, all right, with more reality than she'd ever faced before. Take Vince, for example . . .

No, she couldn't start thinking about Vince. Not today. Not for two weeks, if she could find the strength to keep him at bay.

Thirty minutes later she reached the spot where the crew parked their vehicles. Two pickups were already there. She drew in a big gulp of air. This was it, ready or not. She opened the door and climbed down from the truck to the ground.

Unlocking the door to the office that afternoon, Christy went inside and snapped on the ceiling lights. She shook off her rain jacket and hung it over the back of a chair. She was damp and tired and keyed up enough to scream. They had sent eight loads of logs to the mill, the best day of production since Joe had been hurt. But discovering her own potential for management wasn't quite the kick it should have been.

The men had cooperated and worked hard. Her appearance hadn't seemed to daunt or annoy them at all, although even with the advance notice Clem had given out, a few of the group had been clearly surprised that she'd really shown up.

Nevertheless, the whole crew had listened to her and offered their individual advice, which she'd been glad to get. She now knew each man's capabilities, and which of them could handle more than one phase of the operation. Clem had been so relieved to stop playing foreman that he'd been almost silly.

But Clem had also taken it upon himself to warn her. The conversation hadn't left Christy for a moment since it had occurred.

"Hear you been hanging out with Vince Bonnell," the old man had said casually.

Christy had nearly choked. "I beg your pardon?"

"Just be careful. That's all I'm saying. Bonnell's pretty cagey." Clem had looked around slowly, his gaze moving from one tall Douglas fir tree to another. "I'd bet anything old Vince would love to get his hands on this timber."

The thrust of the startling little talk was twofold: first of all, she was fooling no one. Rock Falls was too small and Vince too well-known for people not to notice his activities. It had to be particularly juicy to the gossips that his latest girlfriend was Joe Morrison's stepdaughter.

Secondly, even Clem knew that Vince would snap up Joe's contract, given the chance. Christy was so guilt-ridden that she was almost ill from it. She couldn't get rid of the image of Vince just lying in the bushes, awaiting the opportunity to spring out and scoop up Joe's contract. And he was keenly aware of every tiny detail of her problems, for which she had only herself to thank.

The day had to go on, no matter how much she wished she could go find a hole to crawl into. Sitting down at her desk, Christy dialed Rennard Lumber Company and asked for Rusty Parnell. He came on the line with, "Damn it, Christy, I've been trying to call you all day!"

She was in no mood for one of Rusty's tirades. "I've been out in the woods. You got eight loads today," she pointed out sharply.

"Well, that's fine, but I need to talk to Joe. I tried the hospital, but there's no phone in his room. Before I drive over to Rock Falls, how's Joe doing? Is he alert enough to talk?"

Apprehension struck Christy hard and fast. "Talk about what?"

"Business."

Christy's breath caught. "You can talk to me about business, Rusty. I don't want Joe bothered with anything right now. I'm holding things together for him, and—"

"I appreciate your position, but Joe's the only one I can talk to about this."

"Then it will have to wait."

"It *can't* wait!"

Christy's voice rose. "Then talk to me about it! Don't you dare come to Rock Falls and bother Joe. If you do, I'll raise so much hell with your boss that you won't know what hit you!"

A moment of stunned silence ensued, and Christy bit her lip, wondering if she hadn't gone too far. Her head was throbbing, her blood pounding. She was under bombardment from every direction, and she'd just about reached the end of her rope. But taking a hard line with Rusty Parnell was dangerous business.

Then she heard a calmer Rusty say, "All right, fine, I'll talk to you. It's about Joe's contract. He's going to be laid up for months, and I've got someone else in mind to take over his job. It would only be temporary, understand. When Joe's on his feet again he can resume the operation, but..."

Christy jumped to her feet. "Wait a minute! No one's taking over Joe's job! I know we haven't been living up to the terms of the contract, but that's all going to change. Eight loads today should count for something. There'll be more tomorrow, and every day from now on."

"I'm sorry, Christy, but it's my job to see that this mill is supplied with a constant flow of timber."

"You have enough timber stockpiled in the mill yard to keep that plant running for years if you never received another load from anyone!"

"I'm not going to argue with a woman about this."

"Don't get sexist on me, Rusty. I found out today that logs and equipment don't give a darn what sex you are."

"Funny."

"I'm not trying to make jokes. This is terribly serious to me and certainly wouldn't speed up Joe's recovery."

"Look, my hands are tied. I've been talking to Bonnell..."

It felt as if a fist had just landed in her stomach. Christy sat down again, landing on the chair hard. "To whom?"

"To Vince Bonnell. He has the manpower and equipment to move in and..."

Rusty kept on talking, but Christy's mind was too numb to absorb the man's words. Vince. Clem had been right. *She'd* been right. Vince had been after Joe's contract all along. She'd known it, but then she'd turned into a fool and allowed charm and sex appeal to get in the way of common sense.

"Do you have a firm deal with Bonnell?" she asked dully when Rusty wound down.

"He said he'd do it if Joe agreed."

"Well, Joe's not going to agree!" Christy shrieked. "And neither am I!"

"But you're not the final word over there, lady. And I'm not so sure Joe *wouldn't* agree."

Christy gritted her teeth. Anger was only making this worse than it already was. She had to calm down. "Look,

Joe's in no condition to face such a decision. If I have to, I'll have his doctor put a no-visitor restriction on his room to keep you out of it!''

"Christy, you can't leave this thing hanging!''

"I don't intend to leave it hanging. The mill is going to be receiving logs every single day from Joe's job. We're going to live up to that contract, and Bonnell has no right sticking his nose in Morrison business! Answer me one question. Did he approach you?''

"I called him. But he said he'd do it, and I think you'd better give the idea some serious consideration. Apparently you think you can run Joe's operation, but you've been doing one hell of a poor job of it. Since the accident, we've received a total of twenty-seven loads of logs. Thirty-five, counting today. That's only about a thirty percent compliance.''

She felt sick to her stomach. "Give me two more weeks, Rusty, this one and the next. Things are running smoother now.''

"Christy...''

He sounded impatient, tired of the argument. "Please, Rusty. Two more weeks. If I don't have things turned around by then, you can give Joe's timber to whomever you please. But if I do, if we're back to full production, I don't want any more conversation about Joe losing his contract. Even temporarily.''

"All right! Two weeks, Christy!''

The telephone was slammed down in her ear. She had infuriated Rusty, which he'd probably never forget, and she'd only won another two weeks. But that wasn't what was killing her. Vince's role in the fiasco was pushing her to the edge of hysteria. How could he agree to take over Joe's job? How could he make love to her with so much emotion and then turn around and arrange a sneaky, underhanded deal with Rusty?

Vince wasn't anywhere near the generous, kind man he had tried so hard to make her believe in. He was just a lot more clever than she was, manipulating her into trusting him, undermining her defenses. His talk about "falling in love" was a line, and boy, had it worked! She didn't have the sense God gave a goose. Tall, handsome children, indeed!

She couldn't bear it. Covering her face with her hands, Christy wept with abject misery. She was the worst kind of fool there was—a woman taken in by an unscrupulous man's innate need to bed every female he met. With his twisted sense of humor he'd probably been laughing up his sleeve all along. Through her he'd been able to keep tabs on Joe's job, and idiot that she was, she had played right into his hands.

Or more accurately, fallen right into his arms.

Her sobs eventually subsided, but nothing would ever diminish the pain in her heart. Vince might have been laying a line on her, but she really *had* fallen in love with him, a horribly harsh fact to realize at this particular moment.

Christy dragged herself to her feet. If the world was going to come to an end unless she turned on that computer, she would merely wait for the blast. Her brain was on stall, and there was no way she could get it functioning enough to concentrate on numbers. She would go home, clean up and then drive over to the hospital, although even that effort seemed overwhelming.

But she had to do what she'd threatened Rusty with: ask the hospital staff to post a No Visitors sign on Joe's door. His recovery wasn't going to be undermined by Rusty Parnell bursting in and insisting on a business discussion, not as long as she had breath in her body.

Or for two weeks, anyway.

At seven that evening Christy walked out of the hospital and across the parking lot to her car. Laura had decided to stay for another hour or so before she went home, because Joe had put in a bad day and she hated to leave him. But Christy had to get up at 4:00 a.m. again the next morning, and Laura had insisted she go home and get a decent night's sleep.

Christy walked with her eyes on the ground. She had concealed her internal agony from her mother and Joe, but it was eating her alive. No one had ever hurt her like this. Her one other go-around with the opposite sex had been milk and honey compared to this feeling of betrayal. She felt used and bitterly unhappy.

"Christy?"

Her mouth literally dropped open. Vince had been leaning against her own car, obviously waiting for her. She had thought about confronting him, but had dreaded what could only be a scene. Now his gall actually weakened her knees.

She stopped in her tracks. "What do you want?" she asked coldly.

"I called the office and your house, then figured out where you must be. Can we talk?"

What was on his face? Guilt? Smugness? What?

She felt suddenly drained. What good would "talking" do? He was too clever for her to pin down in an argument, and he certainly wasn't going to admit what a sneaky snake he was. Christy shook her head and moved to her car. Jerking open the door, she tossed her purse inside. "I don't want to talk."

Vince's face flushed. "This is what I was afraid of. You've talked to Rusty, haven't you?"

She slid behind the wheel of her small sedan. "Go to hell," she said icily, and inserted the key into the ignition. The engine came to life and she pulled the door closed. Without even another glance at Vince, she drove off.

And then, away from the hospital, she began to tremble. The hamburger she'd eaten only half of for dinner was roiling in her stomach with the force of a minitornado. Her hands clutched the steering wheel while she attempted a deep-breathing exercise. If she made it home before being sick, she'd be forever surprised.

How could he? Where did he get his brass? Christy slapped the steering wheel. Did he think she would meekly listen to more of his lies? Maybe he thought she was so dimwitted that she would simper and go find another desk with him!

She hated him. At that moment she hated him so much that every other emotion was blocked out.

Somehow she made it home, and she was even too full of anger to feel relief that she'd gotten there without running into something. Getting out of the car, she slammed the door.

But then she heard the slam of another door, and she whirled to see Vince coming up her walk. "Listen!" he yelled angrily. "You might have a reason to be ticked off, but you have no right to judge me without hearing my side!"

Her eyes blazed. "Get off my property! *That's* my right, Bonnell, to kick off any jerk who steps foot in my yard!"

"You're being ridiculous!"

They were screaming in her front yard, and Christy became aware of it with a stinging humiliation. She spun away, intending to leave him standing there all by himself. Her hand was shaking, but she managed to get the key into the lock. The front door swung open and she ducked inside.

Not quickly enough to elude Vince, though. He followed her in, infuriating her. "Get out!" she screeched. "I swear I'll have you arrested!"

"Just calm the hell down!" He didn't attempt to touch her, although the urge to shake some sense into her was almost irresistible.

"I won't calm down! Get out of my house!"

Vince stood there, sick at heart. "You're the most unreasonable woman I've ever known."

"And ridiculous? How about stupid, Bonnell? And easy? Oh, yes, let's not forget easy! Did you get a big laugh out of yesterday?"

His face was ashen. "No, I didn't get a big laugh out of yesterday. Did you?"

"Me! Now *there's* a reason to laugh." She tried, and failed miserably. "Oh, just go away. Get out of my house...and my life! Who invited you in, in the first place? Who asked you to barge into Joe's affairs?"

She was going strong now. "You planned it all, didn't you? The second you heard about Joe's accident, you saw your opportunity. You rat! Do you think I don't remember how impressed you were with his timber on Saturday?" She mimicked Vince's deep voice, exaggerating his tone. "'Golly gee, Christy, Joe's timber's a lot better than mine.'"

"I didn't say it like that, and I didn't mean it like that, either."

"Oh, yes, you did! You meant it exactly like that. Rusty said he called you, but do you want to know something? I don't believe him. I think *you* called him. I think you suggested he turn Joe's job over to you until poor old Joe recovered enough to take over again." Her voice had turned sickeningly sweet for a moment, then became hard again. "Admit it, Bonnell. Isn't that what happened? And aren't you positive that once you got your hands on Joe's job, Rusty would never take it away from you and give it back to Joe?"

Vince hadn't left the door. He'd been standing with his back to it while Christy ranted in the foyer. Muffin had made an appearance, but had quickly disappeared, a display of uncommon good sense for which Vince could only applaud the little terrier.

"Are you through?" he asked in a lethally quiet voice.

"No! I'll never be through!"

"Well, if I may break in then, have you thought about why you're so quick to think the worst of me? Not just quick, Christy, but eager?"

Her expression became indignant. "Don't try to diminish your guilt by picking apart my motives."

"Maybe your motives need picking apart." Vince tapped his chest. "You see, *I* know what really happened, and all you're doing is guessing. It just seems a little strange that you'd rather scream accusations and insults at me than get to the truth."

"I'm not doing that!"

"No? Think about the past few minutes. Think about that 'Go to hell!' I got in the hospital parking lot. You brought up yesterday, which opens some pretty sensitive doors. Are you afraid of what happened between us? Maybe you'd rather forget it happened."

"Maybe I would," she jeered. But she wasn't screaming now, and she wasn't as positive as she'd been. Not because she believed in Vince's innocence. He was as guilty as sin about wanting Joe's timber. She could almost see him and Rusty Parnell, that jerk, shaking hands on the deal.

But she was hurting terribly, and Vince's line of defense was making her remember. Worse, he had never looked handsomer than he did at this moment, and damn her traitorous soul, she was noticing!

"I don't want to talk about it," she blurted, shaken by her own body's treachery. "In fact, I don't want to talk to you at all! You think you can just barge in here and do anything you want. Well, you can't! Just what makes you so...?"

"What *are* you rambling about? Christy, you're driving me nuts! Do you care? Does it bother you in the least to be pushing a man right to the brink?"

She glared at him, then put her nose in the air and walked into the living room. Vince followed as far as the doorway and slouched against the wooden frame. "I didn't call Rusty. He called me and asked if I could handle both jobs, Joe's and mine, while Joe's laid up. I told him—"

"Stop!" Christy covered her ears. "You're not going to convince me that I've misjudged you." Dropping her hands, she clasped the back of a chair. "Please, leave. I'm tired...and I've got to get up at four in the morning."

"At least you're not screaming at me now," Vince said quietly, walking over to her.

She shivered and blinked back tears. "Just go," she whispered.

His eyes were dark with feelings. He tipped her chin up with a forefinger. "Why would a man want an unreasonable woman?" he murmured, as if asking himself the question.

"Why would a woman want a deceitful man?" she retorted, although with very little vitality.

The pupils of his eyes narrowed in a deep search of hers. "Maybe I was wrong. Maybe we're *not* a couple. Without trust a man and woman don't stand much of a chance."

"I tried to trust you."

"Did you?"

Christy jerked her chin away from his hand. "You *know* I did."

He stood there, and by his expression Christy could tell he was withdrawing. Something flickered and died within her, and life suddenly loomed as very empty. But right was right. She *had* tried to trust him, and received a kick in the teeth for her efforts. "I can't even pretend to understand you," she said in a pain-filled voice.

He sighed. "It's all right, honey. Maybe it was never meant to be. I guess we can look on Sunday as—"

Christy was glad he stopped, because for a second she had feared hearing, "A one-night stand." That was what it was, of course, all it could ever be. So what if it had been the sexual highlight of her entire life? She was a big, all grown-up girl, and it was time she got back into the mainstream. From now on she might be more receptive to dates and getting out of the house, and she had Vince to thank for that turnabout, at least.

He looked as if he was going to walk out the door, and Christy sucked in a tight little breath. As broken hearts went, hers felt smashed into a zillion pieces. If she lived to be a hundred and met an army of men, she would never completely recover from Vince Bonnell.

One corner of his mouth turned up in a cynical grin. "Should we say a proper goodbye, then?"

"A what?"

"Like this." For such a big man Vince could move very quickly, and he scooped Christy into his arms before she could do more than catch on to what was happening and gasp. There were decided disadvantages to being so small, and this was one of them. What chance did she have against a man of Vince's size?

Not that he was hurting her. But he was definitely holding her right where he wanted her, and looking down at her with a challenging light in his eyes. "Kiss me goodbye, Christy."

"Don't be absurd! This isn't a melodrama, you know."

"Kind of feels like one, though, don't you think?"

Why, he was making fun of her! As though she had no right to anger, or worse yet, as though she were only a silly child and should be pardoned for behaving like one.

"Don't you dare treat me like that!" she shouted, furious again.

"Oh, good Lord," Vince muttered. "There's only one way to shut you up." Catching the back of her head in one hand, he brought his mouth down on hers without gentleness or kindness. This was the first purely selfish kiss Christy had ever received from him. He took without giving anything back, forcing her lips apart, pushing his tongue in between.

And then, with an abruptness that left her reeling, he let her go and walked to the doorway. His heavy boot steps continued through the foyer and to the front door. It opened and closed, and the ensuing silence felt almost deadly.

Muffin ran into the room and whimpered at Christy's feet. Tears dripped down Christy's face, and she sank to the floor and put her arms around the little terrier. "Oh, Muffin, everything's in such a mess," she moaned.

Ten

Vince rarely came up against a problem without also seeing some kind of solution. That solution might take work, time, money or a massive headache to carry out, but he'd always felt that most problems were solvable. This thing with Christy had him puzzled, though, until he stopped concentrating on her ridiculous outrage and took a good look at the overall picture.

It came to him right out of the blue while he was shaving late on Saturday morning, after having spent several hours in his yard trimming shrubs, mowing the lawn and cutting wood for the fireplace: Joe!

Vince lowered his razor. One side of his face was still soapy, and he stared at his reflection with his first glimmer of hope since Monday. Why in hell hadn't he thought of Joe before this?

True, this was one of those solutions that would take some doing. Going to Joe Morrison and eating a little humble pie wouldn't be the most enjoyable thing he'd ever done, but without Joe's friendship, what chance did he and Christy really have?

And that was what had been gnawing at him since Monday night—hell, it had been eating chunks out of his hide longer than that: he wanted a chance with Christy. No, not just a chance—he wanted Christy!

Vince laughed almost sheepishly. "Domestic" wasn't his style. It never had been before, at any rate, but he'd been coming up with some mighty peculiar ideas lately. And they had to be due to Christy; there sure wasn't anyone else around to lay them on.

Take his house, for example. He wasn't a great housekeeper by any stretch of the imagination, but the place was comfortable. Recently he'd had stray thoughts about what a woman's—Christy's—touch would do for it. Those green plants in her office stayed in his mind. He could go out and buy some house plants, of course, but the plants were only symbolic of the uncommon turmoil in his system.

This wasn't anything he'd ever experienced before, this sense of incompleteness, of something undone. This feeling of *need*, like a lead weight in his gut.

No, he couldn't stand by and do nothing. It wasn't his way to let problems fester or loose ends just dangle along indefinitely.

Finishing up in the bathroom quickly, Vince pulled on clean clothes and sailed out of the house to his pickup. He drove the shortest possible route to the hospital.

Inside he went directly to Joe Morrison's room and had his hand on the door before he saw the sign. *No Visitors!* Frowning, Vince stepped back. Was Joe worse? What the heck was going on?

Reversing directions, Vince retreated to the nearest nurse's station. He knew the woman on duty. "Leslie, is Joe Morrison all right?"

"Oh, hello, Vince. Joe's doing very well. What's wrong?"

"That sign on his door."

The woman nodded. "Oh, yes. Well, Christy—you know Christy, don't you? Joe's stepdaughter? She requested it."

"Did she say why?"

"Not to me, but then she didn't come to me with the request. I would imagine she went through channels—either the hospital administrator or Joe's doctor."

Vince shook his head at the unexpected hurdle. "I don't get it. You're sure Joe's doing all right?"

"He's got a long way to go yet, but, yes, Joe's doing fine."

"Thanks, Leslie."

Wandering off, moving without haste down a long corridor, Vince tried to come up with a logical reason for that sign. Going over the events since Joe's accident took a few minutes because a lot had happened. Every incident led back to Christy, which he'd already known, but didn't begin to explain why she didn't want Joe having visitors.

Over a cup of coffee in the cafeteria Vince stewed about it. That was what he'd been doing all week—fretting, muttering to himself, snapping at people, functioning with only half of his brain while the other half simmered.

But then it was suddenly so clear that he felt as if some kind of mysterious light had just brightened the room: Joe had no idea what was going on! Christy hadn't only shouldered the responsibility of the business, she'd been keeping Joe in the dark! Damn! Maybe he didn't dare burst in on Joe.

But this couldn't go on. In another conversation with Rusty Vince had learned about Christy's two-week demand. Two weeks was what she'd asked of him, too. What did she think was going to happen in two weeks—a miracle?

One of those weeks had slipped by. How had she done in the woods? Rusty had said that more loads of logs had been coming in from the Morrison job—that second conversation had taken place on Wednesday—but the timber supervisor had still been openly skeptical about Christy handling the job.

"If it doesn't work out, which I'm pretty sure will be the case, will you temporarily take over Joe's job, Vince?" the man had asked.

"I don't know, Rusty. Like I told you before, there are factors that make taking on Joe's job pretty darn touchy."

"You'd be doing him a big favor, man."

"Maybe, maybe not. Let's see what happens, okay?"

Vince took a swallow of coffee. From the very first day of Joe's confinement he'd butted into Morrison affairs. The initial impulse had been because of Joe. After that, everything he'd done had been for Christy.

And this urge to clear the air was because of Christy, too. Yes, she'd be hopping mad about him going to Joe and spilling the beans. But she was hopping mad, anyway, and the way things stood right now, if something didn't change there wasn't a snowflake's chance in hell for Vince Bonnell and Christy Allen ever to be more than residents of the same town.

Face it, Bonnell. You're in love!

The thought had been darting with firefly quickness through Vince's mind all week and then disappearing again into a dense layer of self-preservation. After all, there were moments when it was possible to doubt even liking Christy, let alone loving her. Like during that butt-kicking she'd given him Monday night. Turning her over his knee had seemed very appealing for a few minutes there.

But at the same time he'd understood where she'd been coming from. She was terrified of the situation and fighting her own fears. She was putting up a brave front, but Vince knew that inside she was a teeming mass of self-doubt. Maybe anger was her only defense against the blitz of problems she'd been dealing with.

As for mistrusting him, it hurt like hell that she had such a closed mind. But conditioning was a powerful force, and she had to have heard all her life that the Bonnells and the Morrisons didn't get along.

That feud wasn't funny to Vince anymore. Without that old animosity between the two logging crews, Christy wouldn't have automatically mistrusted him.

Well, brooding about it wasn't doing any good. He had to talk to Joe, and he might as well get to it.

Vince got up, dropped his disposable cup into a trash container and left the cafeteria. He retraced his route back to Joe's room and rapped on the No Visitors sign. Then he pushed the door open.

Laura Morrison was sitting by her husband's bed. Vince sent her a smile and a nod, then he looked at Joe. "Mind if I come in for a few minutes? I think it's time you and I got to know each other."

Having all but ignored Muffin for weeks now, Christy put him on his leash for a walk. She circled the block-size park twice, stopping to let the little terrier sniff at bushes and tree trunks, then sat down at a picnic table under a large shade tree. Muffin was nearby, still on his leash, and very alert to the children playing on the swings and slide some distance away.

It was a rare day. The sky was cloudless, the temperature bordering on hot. Christy was aware of the great weather, but it didn't seem important. Her indifference felt rather sad. Under ordinary circumstances the forever-blue sky would have had her turning mental handsprings.

But nothing going on was ordinary—not events, not her mood. The week had been the most traumatic she'd ever put in, and she was still emotionally involved in it. For one thing, finding out that she didn't like doing Joe's job was deeply disturbing. It wasn't because of the responsibility, but the men humored her, which she hadn't caught on to right away. After a few days, though, she'd started noticing the amusement in their eyes and the masculine condescension in their voices. They were putting up with her, nothing more.

Well, that wasn't quite true. They were also working very hard and putting out a lot more logs than they'd done on their own. So she was good for something besides providing sixteen big macho men with a reason to giggle behind her back.

But she wasn't on the same wavelength with those men. Their sense of humor either floated right over her head or irritated her. They never let up and were either cracking jokes, picking on one another or trying to outdo one of their co-workers in feats of strength. In between cutting down trees and turning them into logs, of course. It was just a different world than she was used to, like some kind of subculture. And she'd thought she was understanding Rock Falls and its residents better? That understanding stopped at the town limits, apparently.

Absently watching the children, Christy sighed. She just wasn't cut out for supervising a crew of loggers. In the past she hadn't seen the men enough to become familiar with any of them. But after only five days they were getting plenty familiar. A few of them saw her small size as cute and had taken to calling her "Peanut."

It was a strange situation—too much familiarity on one hand and respect for her position on the other. The men listened to and followed her recommendations and then laughed at her when they thought she wasn't looking. Apparently they just couldn't take her completely seriously.

Christy had all but given up on Stubb. But the thought of going out to that mountain for six or seven more weeks brought her close to tears. Not only that, her body was creaking and aching in muscles she hadn't even known she'd possessed. She wasn't used to being on her feet for eight hours a day, but she wasn't just standing around out there. She was walking, moving, climbing, stretching, and the aerobics she'd been doing on a fairly regular basis obviously hadn't prepared her body for that kind of activity.

That wasn't a real problem, though. Her aches and pains would pass. Christy restlessly stirred on the picnic table's bench. Why couldn't she stop thinking about Vince Bonnell? *He* was her biggest vexation. Nearly buried under what felt like a mountain of aggravations and worries, Vince Bonnell stood out. Damn the man, he was destroying her! And he was probably going blithely about his daily routines, not giving her so much as a casual thought.

How could she have stumbled into that same trap again? She'd sworn to stay away from egotistical, deceitful men. Vince was exactly like—

No, that wasn't true. As deeply hurt and angry as she felt, Christy couldn't convince herself that Vince was like anyone else she'd ever known. Nor, in all honesty, could she blame him for their lovemaking. She could have said no and she hadn't. That was no one else's fault, not even Vince's.

If only she didn't take everything so blasted seriously. If only she was the type of woman who could make love with a man and walk away humming a happy tune.

Muffin whimpered, then stood up and wagged his tail. Christy glanced down at the little dog, then followed his excited gaze. Vince was walking across the grass, coming their way. Christy's sore muscles tensed, but right along with all of that tension was a dissolving sensation. It was internal—centered somewhere near her heart—and horribly unwelcome. Whatever kind of man Bonnell was, he had become the most important human being in her crazy, upside-down world, and she was in for a long period of recuperation to get over him. A lot longer than Joe's, for that matter.

Vince stopped a few feet away, bent down and scratched Muffin's ears, then straightened again. "Hi."

Flustered, Christy's gaze flitted to his face and then away again. He looked somber, unquestionably uneasy. Where was his overload of confidence? Some of that self-assurance she'd found so discomfiting? "Hello."

"Mind if I sit down?"

She waved a nonchalant hand, as though her heart weren't beating a hundred miles an hour. "Go ahead."

"Thanks." Vince stepped over the bench on the opposite side of the table from Christy. "Great day."

"Perfect weather."

He stared across the table. "How are you?"

She drew a wobbly breath. "Fine." The ensuing pause became uncomfortable, and he kept staring at her. Then, just as she was about to demand that he *stop* staring, he turned his head and looked off at the kids at the other end of the park.

"I have something to tell you," he said quietly.

It was her turn to stare, and she did, through several long moments of wary speculation. Vince finally looked at her again. She was wearing a pink sundress. Her shoulders and throat and arms were bare, except for the inch-wide straps of the dress. Her hair was a mixture of lustrous brown and sunlight, brushing her shoulders, framing her face.

A rush of emotion choked Vince. Not pretty? His initial impression of Christy returned to mock him. She wasn't model or movie star material, but who wanted a showgirl? Christy was the kind of woman thinking men married, certainly the only sort of woman he would ever marry. No damn wonder he hadn't thought of settling down before. The women he'd dated in the past had avoided responsibility like the plague and were only concerned with having a good time.

That was all he'd wanted then, too—a good time. Christy, with her big gray-green eyes hinting at the vulnerability she kept trying to conceal or camouflage with bravado, had completely altered his outlook.

This was what love was, Vince thought, finally admitting and accepting his feelings. Wanting someone so much it was a constant throb in his body, visualizing tomorrow together, and next year, and twenty years down the road. Sharing life, with all of its ups and downs, its joys and disappointments.

But there were no guarantees for him and Christy, not yet. And what he had to tell her was going to cause a strong reaction. Once they got past that they would have the chance he wanted so badly.

He kept his gaze steady. Any sign of disquietude now would indicate uncertainty. And he had to convey conviction that what he'd done was right.

"I just spent an hour with Joe and your mother."

The park suddenly spun for Christy, the ground beneath her feet losing substance. "You what?"

"We had a long talk."

Her thoughts fumbled, searched for something solid. "The sign—"

"I ignored it."

She knew instantly what had taken place—how could she not? The scene was coming at her from every direction. After weeks of painstaking evasion and outright lies, of worrying and even garnering her feeble courage to issue threats to those who would disturb Joe, this man, whom it hadn't even occurred to her might do such a thing, had—

No! Even Vince Bonnell wouldn't do something that low. She couldn't allow her mistrust to go that far. Eluding the worst that could have happened, she went for the obvious. "You went into Joe's room despite the sign. What did you think it was posted for?"

There was a note of hysteria in her voice, and Vince felt his jaw clench. The sign had little meaning right now. "That's beside the point, don't you think?"

She didn't want to hear the point. Stumbling to her feet and untangling herself from the table and bench, Christy tugged on Muffin's leash. Vince stood up. "Running away changes nothing," he stated flatly.

She flashed him a dark glance. "Going to my own home isn't running away. Believe me, every problem in the book is right there in my own living room." She walked off, clinging to Muffin's leash.

"Talk to me, Christy!" He'd thought she would rail at him, which he'd depicted as one more unpleasant but probably necessary chapter in their struggling relationship. But her not allowing the truth to penetrate was worse. There was so much to tell her, if only she would listen. Getting everything back on an even keel had to begin with an open mind, moving on then to discussion and explanation. After that, well, some things were in the hands of the Almighty, and maybe his and Christy's fate was in that category.

When she kept on going, he caught up with her. "I had to start at the beginning, and the beginning was before you were even born."

"I'm not interested."

How cold her voice was, and distant, as though the two of them were complete strangers. No, she would be kinder to a stranger.

"You asked me once how that old feud got started. Do you remember that day?"

Abruptly she turned, spilling out the words that had been choking her, killing her. "How could you? What did you tell Joe? If your interference set his recovery back, I swear I'll—"

"Christy, let me start at the beginning, please. Joe's fine. We talked about a lot of things."

Her eyes were swimmingly bright. "You told him everything, didn't you?" she accused.

"You shouldn't have kept it from him," Vince said softly. "That's his business you've been keeping in operation, Christy. He has every right to know what's been going on."

"That's not for you to say!"

"Is it for *you* to say?"

"I was only trying to protect him. He was in no condition to... to..." Her strength suddenly deserted her. After weeks of fighting her own natural timidity, of forcing herself to summon a courage she didn't really have, of wearing a bold face and attempting to appear plucky and intrepid when she was none of those things, it all quite suddenly deserted her, and she was left with who she really was—an ordinary woman with a hundred frailties.

Before Vince could see her tears of utter hopelessness she managed to show him her back. His startled eyes registered her retreat. "Christy?" There was defeat in the slump of her shoulders and the angle of her head, and every drop of tenderness in Vince's system reached out to her.

He felt pretty defeated, too. Standing there, watching her walking out of his life, he felt like a whipped dog. It hadn't worked. Talking to Joe might have mended some old fences for the two families, but that was all it had done.

Frustration erupted, and Vince slammed a fist into his other palm. No! Damn it to hell, she was the most unreasonable woman he'd ever met, just as he'd told her last Monday night, and he wasn't going to accept that attitude one second longer.

Walking fast, Vince reached Christy at her own gate. "We *are* going to talk," he said fiercely, clamping a big hand on the latch so she couldn't open it. "You pick the place. Right here is fine with me, but so is anywhere else." The moisture under her eyes nearly undid him, but he couldn't let himself go soft now. "Name it, Christy. Here or somewhere else?"

A spark of gumption returned to her eyes. "You have more gall than anyone I've ever known."

"If you're thinking that's an insult, think again."

Her blood pressure was rising. "I really hate you."

Vince swallowed an inward wince. "No, you don't. You're mad and hurt and trying to hurt me back, but you don't hate me."

"You are unbelievably egotistical!"

"Maybe, but I'm also fair and never did want Joe's contract."

"Oh, really?" Her voice dripped sarcasm.

Vince glanced around. "Is this where you want that talk? Fine. I went to see Joe to get a few matters straightened—"

"Just stop! You know darn well I don't want a scene in the front yard."

His eyes narrowed. "Are we going to have a scene? All I'm asking for is about a fifteen-minute conversation."

Her face was flushed, her interior in utter chaos. "Open the gate," she demanded. "You can come in and give your nasty little speech and then I never want to see you again!"

Gritting his teeth, Vince flipped the latch and stood back so she and Muffin could precede him up the walk. Christy heard the telephone ringing before she reached the door. Shooting a venomous look over her shoulder, she hurried on into the house.

The phone in the living room was the closest one. "Hello," she said while doing her best to ignore Vince, who had followed her in.

"Christy? Jeez, you're hard to catch! Joe, too. No one's been at the office, no one's been at home. What the heck's going on out there?"

"Is this Stubb?"

"Sure, it's Stubb. Who'd you think it was? How's everything going?"

Christy stifled an urge to shriek at the man. "May I ask where you are and what you've been doing for almost two weeks?"

"Sure, you can ask. That's what I've been trying to call you and Joe about. I'm at my sister's house in Coeur d'Alene, Idaho. As long as I was in this neck of the woods, I thought I'd drop in on my sis. Say, how come the office has been closed?"

"It hasn't been closed. I just haven't been there very much."

"You been sick or something?"

Vince had sat down on the sofa, but he wasn't making himself at home, Christy noted. He was perched on the edge of the cushion, leaning forward with his arms on his knees, obviously listening. She turned her back on him.

"No, I haven't been sick, but Joe's in the hospital."

"Jeez, no kidding? What happened? Did he have a heart attack or something?"

"He had a bad accident and he's going to be laid up for at least six more weeks. Stubb, I sent you that money to get home on. I was counting on you taking over the logging job as supervisor."

"Jeez, Christy, I'm sorry. I'll get back there as fast as I can. Why didn't you tell me you needed me there when I called before?"

Christy had gone around and around on *that* question so many times that she couldn't bear even thinking about it again. "Just come home, Stubb," she said wearily. "Can I rely on you getting back by Monday morning?"

"Heck, yes! I'll catch the first flight out. By the way, I've got a little news of my own. I quit drinking. Ain't that a hoot? What d'ya suppose the gang will say about old Stubb turning down a beer?"

Amazement and a tremendous relief weakened Christy's knees. She sank down onto the nearest chair, which put Vince right in her line of vision. "Whatever the 'gang' says, Stubb, you have my support and admiration. If there's ever anything I can do, just let me know."

"Hey, that's nice. Maybe we'll do a little talking when I get back. We never did get to know each other, Christy."

After goodbyes Christy slowly hung up the receiver. The atmosphere of her living room was expectant, *Vince* was expectant.

"Stubb's coming home?" he inquired softly.

"Yes. He said he quit drinking."

"Good for him."

It was coming to Christy, gradually at first and then with more speed, that in the space of a few minutes everything had changed. Thanks to Bonnell's unmitigated gall there were no more secrets to keep from Joe, no more reason to sneak around and pretend that everything was wonderful when it wasn't. With Stubb coming home and at least attempting sobriety, she would have a superintendent in the woods. Things were returning to normal, or as normal as they could become with Joe still in the hospital.

It wasn't over yet, of course. There was still Rusty to keep pacified, and if Joe didn't hand down some kind of lecture against secrets, she'd be stunned.

While her burden felt lighter, any relief seemed smothered by discomfiting emotions. Resentment, for one. And righteous indignation. Vince had had no right to go to Joe. He'd crossed a line he shouldn't have even gotten near. Not only had he violated her sense of privacy, he'd intruded on a family matter, both deadly sins as far as Christy was concerned.

"So, talk," she said coolly. "You demanded to be heard. Let's hear it."

"Don't talk down to me, Christy. You've misjudged me from the moment we met, and I'm getting damn tired of your condemnation, your 'I'm a lot more honest than you are' attitude. You're *not* more honest, nor any fairer. You haven't let yourself trust me or really get to know me, and you've based some insulting suspicions and an unjustly negative opinion on gossip and hearsay and the backlash of that old feud." Vince's eyes seemed to grow darker. "We've been at total odds except in one area," he said softly. "We seem to get along just fine when we're making love."

"Which only happened once," she pointed out quickly, sharply.

"Oh, it'll happen again."

"I'm not as sure of that as you are, obviously."

He sat back against the sofa. "I'm *real* sure."

"I thought you wanted to talk." He was making her nervous, looking at her with those gray eyes all heated up and brimming with memories.

"Nothing ever seems to go according to plan when we're together," Vince admitted. "Rather than get into a long, detailed explanation, let's just say that Joe and I worked out our differences. The trouble started between him and my dad about thirty years ago. Both of us are now hoping that our friendship will carry over to our men."

Christy raised a skeptical eyebrow. "You're friends now? Just like that?"

"There never was any reason not to be, not for him and me."

"So after years and years of living in the same town and ignoring each other, the two of you are going to be pals?" Christy rolled her eyes. "I don't believe this."

"Only because you don't want to believe it."

"Anyway, that's not *all* you and Joe talked about!"

Vince studied the resentment on her face. "I told him everything I could think of—what you'd been facing and doing, about Stubb's absence and Rusty's impatience."

"And about your attempt to steal Joe's contract from under *my* nose? Or is that the one point you neglected to mention?"

"I neglected nothing. I explained Rusty's suggestion that I handle Joe's job on a temporary basis, which was all it ever was—a temporary solution. You'd admit it too, if you weren't so damn mule-headed."

"Well," Christy retorted, batting her eyes against the sudden sting of fresh tears. "I guess you put me in my place, didn't you? Proved what a big, strong, take-charge man you are and what a dim-witted, accomplish-nothing woman I am?"

"No one sees you like that, damn it!" Vince exploded. "You've earned everyone's respect, if you'd just open your eyes and take an unbiased look around!"

She blinked for a few seconds, but the tears wouldn't be held back. "I didn't earn *anyone's* respect! Joe's men laugh behind my back, Rusty thinks I'm some kind of idiot, Joe will probably never believe anything I ever tell him again, and you..." Stumbling to her feet, Christy ran from the room.

With a long, drawn-out sigh of resignation Vince got up. Nothing had ever been simple for him and Christy, and why should this be any different? He listened and heard a door slam somewhere in the house, then he walked out of the living room and into the hallway. After a brief hesitation he set out to find her. He wasn't leaving this house until Christy understood everything.

Eleven

———

Vince tried two doors before he found one that wouldn't open. He turned the knob, testing the strength of the lock. Then he put his shoulder against the door and pushed. It gave easily, hardly making a noise.

Christy was on the bed, lying on her stomach. "Go away," Vince heard, a command that was muffled into a forlorn plea by Christy's own arms and the bedding she was huddled into.

He went into the room, barely looking around, and sat on the bed. His hand lifted and settled on Christy's back, a hopeful caress. She cringed away from it, scooting over a few inches.

Vince rubbed his mouth and pondered the situation. Then a thought arose: what the hell? Nothing ventured, nothing gained, and just what did he have to lose? Very casually he stretched out, lying on his back with his head on a pillow.

Then he noticed the room. It had pale yellow wallpaper, fluffy white curtains, a pleasing clutter of feminine trinkets on the dresser, a table, a set of bookshelves. Her bed smelled the way she did—soft and powdery. And the spread beneath his bulk consisted of something lacy.

A grin tugged at his lips. As pleasant as this spot was, it wasn't big enough for him. He thought of kicking off his boots, which were hanging over the foot of the bed, but decided that might be going too far. He noticed a hairline crack in the white ceiling near the light fixture and followed it to the far corner.

"When I was eleven years old," he said quietly, "I got into a squabble with my best friend. We were down at the ballpark. Jimmy was my own age and size, and we argued and fought with each other at least once a week, so one more row was no big deal.

"But some other boys came along, two of them. At the time they seemed like grown men to me and Jimmy, but they were probably around fifteen, sixteen years old. They thought our little brouhaha was funny at first, but then they started pushing us around.

"It was beginning to get nasty when a pickup screeched to a halt. A big man got out and yelled, 'What the hell's going on out here?' He came over and took one of those big boys by the shirt collar. 'Can't you find someone your own size to pick on?' he asked."

Vince chuckled softly. "He gave each of them a light kick in the seat of the pants. 'Get along with you,' he told them. 'And don't let me catch either of you picking on little kids again.'

"Afterward, when we were walking home, Jimmy said, 'That big guy's name is Joe Morrison.' I'd heard the name before, of course, but names of people you haven't met don't mean much to an eleven-year-old. And there was no way I could have met Joe, not when he and my dad went a mile out of their way to avoid each other."

Christy had heard every word, although she'd given no indication of listening. She got off the bed, plucked a handful of tissues from the box on the dresser and blew her nose. Her eyes were red-rimmed and swollen, but she personally didn't give a damn if Bonnell saw her at her worst. She *felt* at her worst—"lower than a snake's belly," as Joe called the mood.

"So Joe didn't know who he'd saved from getting beaten up?" she asked, intrigued by the old tale in spite of more despondency than anyone deserved. Oddly, Vince lying on her bed didn't seem to be that much out of place, not that she was accustomed to seeing a man on her bed. This bed, as a matter of fact, had never felt a man's weight before. She'd bought it new when she moved back to Rock Falls, and she'd been the only person to sleep on it.

Vince settled a level gaze on her. "I'm sure he didn't. I doubt if he even remembers the incident."

"You didn't remind him of it today?"

"We had more important matters to discuss."

Christy leaned against the dresser. "What was the problem between your father and Joe?"

"Some argument over a right-of-way. I honestly don't recall the details. Anyway, it set the tone for the two logging crews."

"Then that feud did start from anger."

"Yes, I suppose it did."

"Why didn't you tell me any of this before?"

Vince sat up, dropping his feet onto the floor. "Would it have made a difference?"

Christy was beyond evasion. "Probably not. It really has nothing to do with the present, does it?" She moved around the room restlessly, rather listlessly. "You've never mentioned your mother."

"She left when I was nine. Married someone else. She lives in a little town near San Francisco. Dad died eleven years later, which was when I took over the business."

"Do you see her?"

"Occasionally. We're not very close."

"That's . . . too bad."

"Yes, it is. But it's the way she wants it. Christy, we have a thousand stories to tell each other."

Her teeth began worrying her bottom lip, while her eyes darted to him and then away again. It happened several times, as though she wanted to look at him but couldn't quite muster up the courage, or whatever it took for her to sustain a gaze.

He patted the bed. "Come and sit by me."

"Why?" she whispered.

"So I can hold you."

"Vince . . ." Her eyes closed.

"You're unhappy and there's no reason for it. Joe's recovering, Stubb's coming home and—" he grinned "—you've got me if you want me."

"I feel so . . . disoriented, I guess. I should go and see Joe."

"Joe's fine."

She walked to the window. "He must be terribly disappointed in me."

"He's proud of you, not disappointed." Vince got up and moved across the room to stand right behind her. She felt him there, big and warm and vital, and shrank within herself a little more. "You took on a heavy load, Christy, and you did okay. Don't look for disappointment where there is none."

"I *didn't* do okay. I tried . . . but nothing really worked out."

Vince looked out the window over her head. "But you're the only one who's disappointed," he said softly. "You kept the job going, Christy. Joe's crew is still intact, he's still got his contract, and with Stubb coming back, you'll have a superintendent."

"We don't know that Stubb can do the job. You said that yourself."

"Yes, I know I did. But I shouldn't have been so quick to judge. Snap judgments can be dangerous."

"Now you're talking about me."

"I'm talking about you and me and anyone else who makes an assumption without any real facts or foundation. I think my biggest concern about Stubb was his drinking. Maybe that's no longer a problem. For Stubb's sake, more than anything else, I hope he makes it."

Christy was trying to pull her disorganized anguish together. Part of it, she realized, was because of a strange emptiness in her system. There were no more secrets now. She could—and would—go to Joe and discuss the business in a practical, forthright manner. His input would be invaluable.

But she had wanted so much to handle it all for him, to relieve him of any possible worry during his convalescence. Maybe she'd been too protective, but everything she'd done had been to preserve Joe's peace.

What she'd overlooked was Vince's audacity. She'd stopped Clem and the rest of the crew from going to Joe, and Rusty Parnell, too. But she'd never even dreamed that Vince might get it into his head to disarm that old feud. It appeared that *any* sort of judgment—hers, in particular—was dangerous.

She still felt betrayed, a sickening sense of having been manipulated and even ignored, as if what she represented was only trivial and not worthy of consideration. "You went around me. You ignored my wishes, my plans, my feelings."

"I knew how you'd feel about it, Christy, but you wouldn't talk to me. Should I have just walked away? That's not how I function."

"No, you honestly believe that you have a right to interfere in other people's lives."

"Look at me." Grasping her shoulders, Vince turned her around. "This all started because of Joe. When I heard about his accident that day, something drew me to the hospital. Maybe I thought about him pulling those two bullies off Jimmy and me—I don't really remember what went through my mind. But I did know positively that if Joe was seriously injured, his business was going to suffer.

"Then I met you and you seemed so sensible. I recall thinking that Joe was lucky to have you working for him. I felt almost immediately that you'd keep everything going, which is exactly what you did do, isn't it? What I didn't expect was the attraction between us. I wasn't looking for that, Christy, and it surprised the hell out of me.

"You fought it every step of the way. You decided at first sight that I wasn't to be trusted, and nothing I said or did got past that wall of doubt. Then I realized that I wasn't trying to help out because of Joe anymore. It was because of you. I cared what happened to you. I cared when you were hurting, and I cared about your fears and your lack of confidence with Joe's crew. I *cared,* Christy. I still do."

Her eyes were enormous, staring up at his face with a stunned expression. "You went to see Joe *because* of me?"

"I did it for both of us. If Joe and I continued to avoid each other, how would you and I ever get past first base? I know how close you are to Joe and your mother, and you've done everything but turn inside out to keep our relationship private."

"It didn't work. People are talking."

"Exactly. Well, I want everything out in the open. I want to take you places and not give a damn about who sees us or what anyone thinks about it. I want us to spend time together, to talk and tell those stories, and go anywhere we please without worrying that it might get back to Joe."

"Did . . . you say that to Joe and Mom today?"

"I let them know I was interested, yes."

She searched his eyes, probing their most private corners. There was nothing there she hadn't seen before, except that maybe the affection and warmth and kindness were a little more intense. He seemed to be telling the truth; maybe he really did care for her! It was an astonishing revelation, a complete reversal of everything she had suspected him of.

"I've told you what I want. How about you doing the same?"

She wasn't sure she could, not with the blistering humiliation she was experiencing. How could she have been so blind, so locked into one narrow perspective?

"I don't know what to say," she whispered, uncertainty in the feeble attempt even to speak.

The silence of the house had been seeping into Vince's consciousness. They were completely alone, except for Muffin, who'd wandered into the room at one point and then back out again after a bored yawn.

"Maybe we've talked enough for now," Vince said softly, running his hands downward from her shoulders to her slender wrists. The straps of her dress looked like strips of pink taffy against her skin, inviting a taste. Everything about her suggested and invited, for that matter. His response to Christy was only what he'd come to expect in her presence—emotional awareness of her special blend of femininity accompanied by uncontrollable physical urges.

Wondering if she would ever be sure enough of herself to make the first overture in lovemaking, he raised her hands to his lips. Their eyes met over a kiss to one palm, and he saw hers widen in sudden understanding of what he was doing. "Don't withdraw," he whispered. "Let go of that wall. It's vanishing. Let it."

If she made love with him now, her fate would be sealed. Was that what she wanted—to forgive and forget and accept that everything he'd done had been for her? For them? It was the simplest path and surely the most desirable. But some small part of Christy rebelled at complete surrender.

Only the rebellion didn't quite reach whatever it was in her own makeup answering Vince's call. His touch evoked sensation, an overwhelming tingle that took her system by storm and spread even to her toes, her fingers. Its core, the center of her being, was instantly hot and palpitating, trembling in anticipation.

He released one hand to stroke her hair, moving then to trail his fingertips along her cheek, the indentation of her throat, across a shoulder. He bent and placed a kiss within an especially tempting hollow at the base of her throat, where he could see the fluttering rhythm of her pulse. He wanted her with him, as she'd been the day they'd made love on her desk. He wanted her to match his own wanting, to need what he needed, to feel what he was feeling.

Christy saw his desire in the smoky intensity of his eyes. Where they were—her bedroom—was significant, but she could stop everything with one word. She could say no and watch the flames in his eyes turn to ashes. But without Vince Bonnell nothing seemed to have much meaning. She'd already learned that lesson in the past week.

Nothing was certain in life, which she'd known for a long, long time. Childhood was only a series of dim memories, but since Joe's accident she had felt as insecure as an unwanted child, which was almost incomprehensible. Had she been so glued to her smooth little rut that a bumpy detour caused panic?

Possibly, but what had caused her need of Vince? Loneliness? Believing herself contented, and satisfied with mostly her mother, Joe and Muffin for company when she hadn't been? Christy gazed up at Vince and absorbed each tiny subtlety of his face. He smiled, and the creases at each side of his mouth deepened, while the crinkles at the corners of his eyes became more visible. She felt defenses that were already weakened crumbling even more.

She dropped her head to his chest and became instantly aware of the hard beat of his heart. Big arms closed around her, and she felt Vince's face in her hair. "Christy, honey, the worst is over. Believe that. Believe in me. Stop torturing yourself."

She dampened her lips. Her cheek was pressed to Vince's chest, nestled into his shirt and the muscles beneath. "Maybe it's myself I need to believe in," she whispered.

"What? I didn't hear you. What did you say?"

She wrapped her arms around his waist. "It wasn't anything important." Standing on tiptoe, she nestled closer. It was all the cooperation Vince needed, and he groaned and sought her lips. His mouth coaxed, caressed, teased hers with an urgent pressure. Sweet desire careened through her system, a heady replacement for the traumatic effects of the day, easing doubts, fears and disappointments.

She sank into the kiss; she could feel herself doing it, which was logically impossible when he was so much bigger. *He* might be able to sink, but she was stretched out to her full height and then some. Still, she sank, or felt as if she did. Her insides, anyway.

Her lips parted for his tongue, which delivered another sinking sensation. And thrill upon thrill compounded until she was kissing him back with enough fervor to rock him back on his heels.

Her response was everything Vince had hoped for. He cupped her face between his hands and rained kisses over her face, on her nose, her eyelids, her lips. "Christy..." His voice was as rusty as old nails. "Baby...you know I love you, don't you? You know this isn't just fooling around for me, don't you?"

The words penetrated the fog of her brain, or started to, before she shut them out. Later, maybe. After she'd had a little time to digest the day, after she'd talked to Joe and heard his opinion of Vince's brashness. Her own caution seemed overly amplified, but there was that one small spot of rebellion yet to pacify.

"Christy? Did you hear what I said, honey? I love you." He held her away from him to look at her face.

She couldn't meet his eyes. "I...heard."

Something powerful and painful shot through Vince, a ripping dread. He loved her, but there were no guarantees, none, that she would love him back. Doubting their sexual chemistry was impossible; it was all around them, heating and even scenting the room. But dear God, why hadn't he anticipated the possibility of Christy finding him only sexually appealing and to hell with the rest?

He brought her close again and shut his eyes. His breathing was ragged, his pulse erratic. He could make her love him; he knew he could. His hands moved up and down her back. She was so small, so perfect. No other woman would ever do, no matter how beautiful, how confident, how sure of herself she might be.

Any trace of cockiness he'd ever been guilty of was completely gone, erased as if by magic. His body molded to her smaller form as though it were a precious jewel. He tipped her chin, and his kiss was as delicate as rose petals, tender, gentle, conveying all of the love in his heart and soul.

Her lips parted with a soft, sighing sound. She was up on her toes and still not tall enough to direct the essence of the kiss. Maybe she'd hurt him by her reluctance to talk about love, but she hadn't meant to.

"Kiss me for real," she whispered, deeply shaken by what she felt from him.

He was so hard, he ached. She was an enigma, this tiny woman, private and wary and yet so ripe and sensual. He couldn't stop himself; the tenderness of his kiss suddenly became demanding. His hands wove into her hair, grasping handfuls, while his tongue plunged into her mouth.

From her hair his fingers slid down to her shoulders, and the straps of her dress were quickly eliminated. The kissing never stopped, one requiring another, each one more breathy than the previous. He was bending over, she was balancing on her toes, and there was more than enough space between their straining bodies to reach each other's clothing.

She plucked at the buttons on his shirt, and he struggled with the mysteries of her dress. How did she get into it? And out of it? It had no buttons, no zipper.

"Like this," she gasped, and simply pushed the entire dress down and stepped out of it. His gaze devoured her. She was braless and wearing only a wisp of pale pink bikini panties. Staring at her, he quickly disposed of his shirt. Christy went to the bed and threw the spread back. She drew the blanket and the top sheet down, then turned to watch him undress.

With his hips against the dresser he yanked off his boots and socks. His shirt was already on the floor, and she was lost in the wonder of his magnificent chest. He unbuckled his belt, and her breath caught in her throat. This was very much like their passion in the office that day, but different, too. The bed lent intimacy to the excitement they were both experiencing, and she felt much bolder than she had then.

That boldness was an internal thing, because externally, how could she be any less inhibited than she'd been that day? It was because she knew things about him this time, Christy breathlessly decided. She knew that he was utterly beautiful naked, and that he would use protection, and that he would see to her pleasure before his own.

Her breasts moved with her breathing, her nipples upright and sensitive. She licked her lips when he reached for his zipper, then brushed a tangle of hair from her face, both gestures laden with anticipation.

Vince saw it all—how she was waiting for him, how ready she was. His body was taut with tension, the muscles of his arms and chest nearly as rigid as his manhood. But he dragged out the moment, unabashedly hoping it would release her pent-up feelings. That was all her reluctance was, he told himself, only her natural resistance to revealing her inner self. He was used to that with Christy, wasn't he? He'd get past it. Somehow he'd get her talking.

She was only about three strides away. He reduced the distance by a few feet and slowly slid the tab of his zipper about halfway down. Her expression was pure fascination. He moved closer. "You do it."

Her gaze jumped to his face. "Me?"

He hooked his forefingers into the elastic band of her panties. "Do you want to do it? You have to tell me what you want, Christy?"

She wasn't afraid, only surprised. She'd been thinking that she'd known how he made love, and she didn't. One experience with Vince hadn't made her any kind of expert. She took a tantalizingly long breath, which brought Vince's total attention to her bare breasts. "I want to do it," she admitted, mesmerizing Vince with her husky whisper.

His hands slid up her body and stopped, one on each breast. His eyes dared and challenged while he caressed and stroked her pouty nipples and warm, firm flesh.

Her legs nearly gave out from the pleasure of his touch, but she licked her lips again and reached for his zipper. It wasn't possible to touch it and not feel what was behind it. His maleness was hot and heavy and stretching seams. He was playing with her, she sensed, testing her.

He was forever testing her, it seemed, pushing her beyond her own limits in one way or another. Would she have even thought of going into the woods without him badgering her into it? Who else had ever tried her emotions the way Vince did?

She suddenly wanted to shock him, to shake his self-confidence. He had no right to manipulate her the way he was always doing. His personality was stronger than hers, and he constantly used his advantage to outsmart her. Bringing Vince Bonnell to his knees, at least once, was necessary to her mental health. This seemed like a most auspicious time to assert herself, to show him that she fully intended to maintain control of her own destiny, wherever their relationship took them.

"Ahh," she whispered, splaying her hand upon the heated bulge of his fly. "What have we here?"

Response to her touch shot throughout Vince's body. He gulped a huge lungful of air. Intense pleasure fired his hunger when she seductively caressed him, first through his pants, then without them. The zipper had been quickly dispensed with, of little consequence, after all. Her small hands encircled and stroked, and she leaned forward to dampen his chest with her tongue.

He closed his eyes and let the pleasure flow. This was how he wanted her, confident, unafraid to express whatever she was feeling. If she could do it in the bedroom, she could do it elsewhere. Her kisses, the touch of her hands, were feather-light, sensually tormenting.

It all felt fabulous, incredible, but he wouldn't last another three minutes. He wrapped his arms around her and brought her too close for that kind of stimulation to continue. Her skin seemed to singe his, the peaks of her breasts on his chest causing nearly intolerable excitement. She snuggled and rubbed against him, and pushed his pants and briefs down past his hips.

His heart was pounding hard enough to hear. They weren't even on the bed yet, and he was on the verge of—

He had to calm down, or it would be over before it really began. She was a vixen, a coquette, a tease. Her hands wouldn't be still, her kisses fell indiscriminately. And then he heard, "You have to tell me what you want, Vince."

He stiffened, recognizing his own words. His eyes darkened. The balance of power was moving back and forth between them. That she would deliberately insinuate their ambiguous bond into their lovemaking was staggeringly meaningful: she wouldn't be controlled, and he'd been pushing too damn hard!

At least she'd gotten her point across without anger. In fact, what he was feeling from her was as hot as a firecracker and satisfyingly durable. She loved him, all right, only everything wasn't quite settled in her mind.

"Suppose I show you," he whispered hoarsely, and let go of her to kick his pants and briefs away. Still playing the temptress, Christy stripped off her panties. They both scrambled for the bed at the same time.

"Show me," she taunted, lying on her back and holding her arms up to him. And then, when he gathered her into a fierce embrace, intending no gentleness, for that was what she'd driven him to, she whispered softly, "Show me, Vince."

Breathing hard, he held her, with closed eyes and a silent prayer for endurance. She'd brought him higher than a kite, then back down to earth. She was asking for love now, not just an expression of desire. So be it.

He caressed her body in long, slow strokes of contained passion. His mouth nibbled at hers, his tongue darting within for delicious forays and then out to her lips. He kissed her breasts, lingering on each turgid crest until she moaned in the back of her throat.

She caught his hand and brought it down to the unbearable ache between her thighs, and when he touched her, she cried out with ragged, wrenching desire.

There was no struggle for power now. They only wanted, needed. Perspiration lay on their skin; they were breathing in gasps. And then Vince could take no more. In the next instant he was on her, in her, moving within the satin of her body, reveling in her heat, rejoicing in her moisture.

Her glazed eyes looked into his. "I love you," he whispered. "I love you."

And finally he heard what he'd known to be true all along: "I love you."

Everything was left behind then. Thought and reason and every faculty but sensation vanished into a maelstrom of all-consuming passion.

Twelve

Christy hadn't given an unequivocal yes to Vince's proposal of marriage, and on Sunday she was haunted with the whys of her reluctance. All during a long talk with Joe, a few minutes with her mother and a short session with Stubb—yes, the wandering boy had finally come home— Christy was all too aware of a deeply rooted personal discomfort.

She loved Vince; she'd even told him so. He loved her, too, and had been generous with praises and plans. But something wasn't quite right. She had an inner uneasiness and hadn't participated very eagerly with Vince's enthusiastic ideas for their future together.

He'd known it, of course. The man was too keen-minded and perceptive not to have seen through her ambivalent responses. But she couldn't completely overlook the stormy side of their relationship, which Vince seemed to be doing, or pretend that those old arguments weren't still affecting her.

That afternoon Christy left the hospital and, in her own small sedan, headed out of town. The Pacific Ocean was only about twenty miles away, but she would go to a favorite spot, Knotts Bay, which added another twelve miles to the trip. The extra distance was insignificant. She needed to think, and driving alone would give her the opportunity.

She found no answers during the drive, only more questions. Or rather, a dozen variations of the same question: why, if she truly loved Vince, was she hesitant about going forward with their relationship?

At Knotts Bay she took off her shoes and walked in the surf. A few fishermen were about, a few strollers, some sunbathers. The day was beautiful, as yesterday had been. Gulls swooped and screeched, gentle breakers washed the beach, and Christy walked along slowly, achieving a sense of serenity, as she always did near the ocean.

She stayed an hour, then, with her mind clearer, returned to her car and drove back to Rock Falls.

Vince lived on Norris Road, which was about a mile from the northern limits of town. Christy had always known which house was his, and she drove directly to it. She saw at once that Vince was home—his pickup was parked in the driveway. When she pulled her car up behind it, she spotted him coming around the back of the house, carrying a hammer and a short piece of lumber.

She turned off the engine and got out. He was walking toward her and wearing an apprehensive expression, as though he expected to hear bad news. "Hi," she said.

"Hi." He bent and placed a kiss on her lips, sending a starburst of sparks throughout Christy's system. But she hadn't come here just for kisses, and she kept her emotions in check. Vince felt her restraint. "Everything all right?"

"I think it could be with a little conversation." She saw the concern in his eyes. She was worrying him, she knew, but it couldn't be helped.

"Sure, I'd like to talk, too. Let's go inside."

He dropped the hammer and board at the back door and escorted her through a utility room and into his kitchen. Christy took a glance around. The room was well equipped and clean, but bland. Vince wasn't much for frills, apparently. A woman's touch would do wonders. Was she really going to be the woman to decorate Vince's house?

"How about something to drink? Iced tea, cola, a beer? Or I could make a pot of coffee."

Christy realigned her wandering and very unsettling thoughts. "Iced tea will be fine, thanks."

He took ice and a pitcher from the refrigerator and filled two glasses, darting her uncertain looks in the process. "Been to the hospital?"

"I spent some time with Joe this morning. Stubb, too. He's back and seems determined to stay sober."

"Good for him." Vince offered a faint grin. "Good for you, too, huh? With him on the job you won't have to go back out to the woods."

Christy accepted the glass he handed her. "Hopefully."

"Let's sit in the living room."

"Fine."

It took a few minutes to get settled, her on the couch, Vince on a large leather chair. They both took a drink of tea and smiled tentatively at each other.

"I drove over to Knotts Bay after I left the hospital," Christy told him. "I've always found the ocean soothing."

Vince hesitated, then asked, "Did you need soothing, honey?"

"I needed to think, Vince."

"About us."

"Yes."

His eyes looked terribly sad. "Don't you want to marry me, Christy?"

She looked down at the glass in her hands. "You pulled the rug out from under me yesterday, Vince. I was so engrossed in the business and helping Joe, and then, all at once, it was all gone."

Vince frowned. "All gone? I don't follow you. What was gone, Christy?"

"That's what I had to figure out. There was this enormous hole...." She laughed weakly. "I know this sounds strange."

"No, please go on."

"I felt...disconnected, I guess. I had been handling things—badly, I'm the first to concede. But—"

"You did a helluva job. No one could have done any better."

She raised an eyebrow. "*You* could have done better, Joe could have done better, maybe even Clem could have, if he'd been willing to put out the effort. Vince, *lots* of people could have done better than I did. But I gave it a hundred percent. I tried, and I sincerely believed that keeping the problems from Joe was best. That became my primary goal—to protect Joe."

He was watching her closely, searching her every word for meaning, studying its shadings, deciphering what it meant to her, what she was attempting to convey. And he began to understand. Her protectiveness had been like a special gift to Joe. At whatever expense to herself she'd assumed the role of guardian. Eradicate that noble cause, which Vince knew he had done, and she was left with only a tough job.

"I see now what I destroyed yesterday," Vince said quietly. "Christy, I only went to Joe to mend that old breach. I wish you and I could have talked first."

"I think you tried," she said with a feeble smile, admitting that she'd been uncooperative that night.

"Probably not hard enough." Vince got up, set his glass on an end table and walked over to the sofa, sitting down beside Christy. "So, what is it you want to do, honey?" he asked.

She turned her head and looked directly into his eyes. "Wait."

"Wait," Vince repeated softly. "Wait for what?"

"Wait to get married. Yesterday you were talking about doing something very soon. I want to wait until Joe's back to work, and until..."

"Until you're a little surer of me?"

Her gaze probed his. "Are you so sure of me?"

"I'm sure that I love you. Is loving each other what we're talking about? It's not, is it? What is it, Christy? What are you afraid of?"

She didn't want to accuse. What was done was done, but Vince rushed into things, like going to Joe without understanding all of the implications of his actions. He was a take-charge man, just as she'd told him yesterday, which was great in many ways but not necessarily an asset in marriage.

"I'm afraid of you," she said softly. At his show of surprise she added quickly, "You're impetuous, Vince, and I'm not. I have to weigh things from every angle. You get an idea and jump right smack into the middle of it. Like going to Joe yesterday. Did you hesitate even once and ask yourself how I might feel about it?"

He reached out and touched her hair, brushing it back from her cheek, curling a strand around his forefinger. "I asked myself, 'Vince, what will Christy think of you going to see Joe?' And I answered, 'She'll be hopping mad, that's what'll happen.' But I went, anyway, because without Joe's friendship, you and I didn't stand much of a chance. That might have been impulsive, but with you sitting here talking about marriage, I can't find it in myself to regret it, Christy."

"You're saying it worked and that you'd do it again."

"In a heartbeat."

She looked at her glass again. "That's my point, Vince. We're different kinds of people. I could no more barge into someone else's business than I could fly, and 'barging' is second nature to you."

"And you think that's some sort of insurmountable obstacle between us and a happy marriage?" Vince took her free hand and held it with both of his. "I guess this is something you have to work out, Christy. I'm who and what I am, just as you are. If I was seventeen, I might be able to change, but I'm thirty-six. I think my personality is pretty well set, don't you?"

Was that what she was doing, asking Vince to change? Christy frowned.

"Christy, do you trust me now? Do you believe that it never once occurred to me to go after Joe's contract, and that everything I did, or tried to do, was because of Joe and you and not for what I might get out of it? I can't prove it, you know. It's a matter of you looking back and taking what happened at face value. Of believing instead of doubting."

When she made no reply and seemed to be pondering his words, Vince went on. "You want to know what had me worried when I realized how attracted I was to you? You're a classy lady, Christy. You're educated and smart and so far above an old lumberjack like me that I was afraid you wouldn't give me the time of day."

Her startled gaze flew to his face. "You're not serious." But he was; she could see it in his eyes. With all of his self-assurance and certainly more nerve than anyone else she'd ever met, he was also capable of self-doubt.

A wash of emotion brought tears to her eyes. She'd been cautious with men ever since her big fiasco in Seattle, but stubbornly looking for hurdles—obstacles—to keep herself from committing to a warm, generous and incredibly kind human being was becoming ridiculous.

"I trust you," she told him tearily, barely able to speak above a whisper.

"Come here." Vince pulled her onto his lap, snuggling her firm little body close to his chest. "Honey, I'll try to stay out of your personal business, but if anything threatens you in any way, I'll have to interfere. That's just the way I am."

Christy buried her face in the curve of his neck and shoulder. "I do love you," she said with a sob. "And I trust you. I really do. I'm sorry I was such a..." She searched for the right word, but couldn't come up with one to describe accurately how she'd behaved.

"Pain in the neck?" Vince suggested with a small chuckle.

She found herself laughing. "Pain in the neck" had to be right on the money, from Vince's point of view. Actually, he could have pinpointed a much lower portion of the human anatomy and still been correct. Looking back at his almost constant efforts to help and her own unrelenting ingratitude, she must have driven him crazy.

Love had to be a very powerful force to endure and flower despite so many impasses.

Vince was stroking her hair and back. "Do you still want to wait to get married?"

Christy sat up and wiped her eyes. "I'd like Joe to take part in the wedding."

"I'd like that, too. We'll wait until he's well enough. In the meantime..." His fingers moved to the buttons on her blouse, and looking into his eyes, Christy saw the smoky drift of desire.

She smiled and began working a button loose on his shirt.

Epilogue

The wedding reception was held in the Rock Fall's community center, the only place in town big enough to accommodate so many guests. There was music, a three-piece local band that specialized in country and western, tables of food, kegs of beer, soft drinks of every flavor and the most beautiful wedding cake Christy had ever seen.

Vince wore a pale blue tuxedo and looked so handsome that Christy couldn't keep her eyes off him. Her dress, made of ivory satin and lace, was gorgeous. The ceremony had been perfect. Joe and Laura were beaming as if lit by inner bulbs. The guests were dancing, eating, drinking and having a marvelous time.

But the Bonnell people sat on one side of the hall and the Morrison people on the other. Christy kept trying to ignore the guest placement, but every time she looked at the crowd, the division gave her a pang.

Vince, who'd been talking to someone, came up and dropped his arm around her shoulders, squeezing her to his side and giving her a kiss on the lips. "You look beautiful in that dress, honey," he whispered. "So why do I keep thinking about getting you out of it?"

She laughed softly. "Probably for the same reason I've been imagining you without that blue tux."

"Do you think we could slip away for a few minutes? There are several unused rooms in this building."

Christy laughed. "Patience, my love." The music and laughter swirled around them. "Vince..."

"Yes?"

"You've noticed what's happening here, haven't you?"

He looked the room over. "Yeah, I've noticed. Don't let it worry you, honey. Everyone's having a good time."

It *was* worrying Christy, though, and the whole thing was so silly. With Joe and Vince friends, why would their men cling to that old feud? Throughout the festivities Christy kept a wary eye on the crowd. Those men had engaged in fistfights on more than one occasion, and with their penchant for getting ahead of their competitors one way or another, anything was apt to happen.

Stubb was wandering around the Morrison side of the room with a soft drink can in his hand. Bless him, Christy thought with genuine fondness. He'd no doubt gone through hell with his battle against the bottle, but he hadn't slipped off the wagon even once. And he'd handled the woods and kept Rusty Parnell happy, which was no small feat. Joe was back to work now, but he'd appointed Stubb his permanent foreman and was taking it a little easier than he used to.

This was unquestionably the happiest day of Christy's life. She loved Vince so much that the emotion filled every nook and cranny of her body. Joe was well, Laura was ecstatic, the business was in good shape and the future looked serenely blissful.

Except for that invisible line down the center of the hall, everything was perfect.

"Dance with me, Mrs. Bonnell," Vince said softly.

Christy's heart fluttered. "I'd love to."

Vince led her onto the dance floor, and they took up the slow rhythm of a pretty ballad. As they turned, Christy's eyes widened. "Oh, my Lord," she whispered. "Vince, look at that."

"At what?" He craned his neck and saw Stubb crossing the room toward Bonnell territory. "Oh-oh. What's going on?"

An air of expectancy seemed to invade the entire hall, as if everyone present had started holding their breath. "Well, I'll be damned," Vince exclaimed quietly.

"He asked Myrna Cartwright, your secretary, to dance! And she accepted!" Excitement drained Christy's tension. "Vince, she accepted!"

And then, right before their very eyes, a small miracle unfolded. Bonnell people got up from their chairs and Morrison people left theirs. They asked one another to dance. They talked and shook hands. They slapped backs and laughed.

Christy's eyes filled with tears, and she couldn't stop her lower lip from trembling. Vince drew her closer. "It's over, honey. That old feud's a thing of the past."

His voice had been choked; he was as emotional about this as she was, Christy realized. She began laughing, just a small teary hiccup at first, but it expanded and grew until it contained joy and gladness and bubbled from her lips like the fizz of fine champagne.

Laughing, too, Vince lifted her and spun her around and around until they were both dizzy.

Everything was right with the world—absolutely everything!

* * * * *

This is the season of giving, and Silhouette proudly offers you its sixth annual Christmas collection.

SILHOUETTE

Christmas Stories

1991

Experience the joys of a holiday romance and treasure these heartwarming stories by four award-winning Silhouette authors:

Phyllis Halldorson—"A Memorable Noel"
Peggy Webb—"I Heard the Rabbits Singing"
Naomi Horton—"Dreaming of Angels"
Heather Graham Pozzessere—"The Christmas Bride"

Discover this yuletide celebration—sit back and enjoy Silhouette's Christmas gift of love.

Angels Everywhere!

Everything's turning up angels at Silhouette. In November, Ann Williams's ANGEL ON MY SHOULDER (IM #408, $3.29) features a heroine who's absolutely heavenly—and we mean that literally! Her name is Cassandra, and once she comes down to earth, her whole picture of life—and love—undergoes a pretty radical change.

Then, in December, it's time for ANGEL FOR HIRE (D #680, $2.79) from Justine Davis. This time it's hero Michael Justice who brings a touch of out-of-this-world magic to the story. Talk about a match made in heaven . . . !

Look for both these spectacular stories wherever you buy books. But look soon—because they're going to be flying off the shelves as if they had wings!